Gallois and The Pit of Lost Souls

Patrick A. Hunter

Acknowledgements

I WOULD LIKE to thank God for his grace, mercy and for blessing me with a loving and supportive family. To my Mom, Anita, Shonta and my five beautiful nieces, I love you all.

Chapter I

FABIAN'S EYES FLUNG open to find that he was surrounded by darkness. For a moment he panicked, thinking that those he feared had found him and killed him in his sleep. But then he felt the firm of wood against his backside and bed mattress beneath him.

He remembered he had turned out the light supposedly just for a few minutes until his wife had fallen asleep. He let out a weary sigh and felt stupid for having the thought of being killed so quickly; a quick death was never the case with the Nesphar. With heavy eyelids, he turned and looked down at the patch of darkness he knew to be Heather sleeping next to him, resting comfortably in the belief that she was as safe as she was loved.

Moving slowly, he reached over and gently moved aside a few strands of her raven hair to reveal the full side of her oval face. She was undeniably beautiful with radiant, caramel skin, a petite frame and brown eyes that would have made Cleopatra herself jealous. He was certain that had she lived centuries ago she would have been the wife of some jealous king. In these times, even though she was approaching thirty, she could be a model or an actress if she wanted but he knew she would hear no word of pursuing anything that glorified her beauty because it had been the cause of much of her childhood pain, the type of pain that he vowed to never let befall her again.

He cursed himself for having fallen asleep. Fatigue was a difficult adversary, especially after working a twelve-hour shift unloading cargo trucks with a forklift, but he would not let it beat him.

He looked to his right at the small green light of the baby monitor on the nightstand, realizing the slow rhythmic sounds of his five year-old son Gallois sleeping had most likely helped sway him to sleep. Then he checked the time on the digital clock next to monitor, 2:46 a.m., just over fifteen minutes since he had last checked and well within the Witching Hour, as those who hunted him called it.

He shook his tired head, thinking about how foolish it was for people to be attracted to darkness or to believe that loyalty to anything of it would be returned or rewarded. If they understood it, they would know that evil has no loyalty. He had not been so reckless. Instead, he had been born into it, born to live in darkness, and up to six years ago he had done so happily.

Things were different now. He had a new life and new enemies in the Nesphar, a satanic cult from seventeenth century Europe. With over a million followers spread throughout the world. They were far less threatening than the evil to which they aspired to, but they were ruthless and enthusiastic students known for assassinating those who opposed them during the Witching Hour, as an offering to waiting demons.

For years Fabian had been certain that he was off the Nesphar's radar. But that all changed four nights ago when an icy chill woke him from a sound sleep. He had felt that chill ever since, Death's cold breathe on the back of his neck. At first, he tried to disregard the sensation as worry, one of the many things he had to get used to. But he knew better. Something was coming for him, slithering from the darkness to steal life from him.

He hoped that they would not come for him this night. Tomorrow he was going out of town on a faked month long outsourcing job. He would not return until he was certain that his family was safe. He hated lying to Heather, but he needed the time to check his connections and leave a false trail.

He felt Heather's arm fall into his lap. Her soft, comforting body stretched over his legs. He slowly sat up higher, preparing to inch away from her. He had not told her. Heather never took well to stress, and she would surely be much more of a wreck than he was right now. He slid free of her arm, maneuvered his sizable frame to the side of the bed, yawned, and scratched at the stubble that was itching his face. The sight of the balcony door cracking open scared him stiff. Was the evil already in the room with them?

He dared not move, or breathe as he wondered at the thin beam of moonlight reflecting off the wooden floor. Surely he had not slept hard enough not to notice someone slipping into the room. His heart skipped a beat as the door slowly moved toward him and the glow of moonlight widened.

He reached for the shotgun underneath the bed. His finger was on the trigger and barrel aimed the door when a faint whistle of wind revealed itself as the only intruder. He lowered the weapon, but still the mystery was not solved. He arose to check the balcony, stepping over his blue slippers with words #1 Dad painted on them in a red and brown scrawl. Cool air and sounds of traffic met him as he pulled open the balcony door.

After a quick, careful survey, he found the balcony empty. He checked the door latch. It appeared undamaged, but he would change it before for he left tomorrow. He glanced at the clock again. Only a few minutes had pasted.

Maybe some fresh air would help. He moved in the direction of the balcony railing, and a warm clam rushed through him. All his worries, fears, and doubts began to fall away, taking with them the tension in his face and neck. Within seconds, all felt right in the world and with him. Standing there with a broad smile and watery eyes he realized that, while memories of his previous life were fading fast as they did for all descended, he still knew the sense of peace that signaled the presence of his brothers and sisters.

He strolled to the balcony railing. "I can still feel your presence Victor," he said to open air as his eyes roamed the balcony. "Come on, let me see you. I know you're here."

Silence answered.

He sighed. "Okay. I suppose I don't have to see you in order to talk." He leaned over the balcony's concrete railing and rested his weight on his forearms. He gazed far into the distance, at the towering sky-scrapers beyond the neighboring apartments.

His eyes settled on the Empire State Building, the closest of all the others and the last place he remembered conversing with Victor all those years ago.

"It's been quite some time since you've visited me," Fabian said. "I won't pretend not to know why. But please believe me brother. My only regret of this new life is that it made you feel betrayed. I hope this visit means you've finally forgiven me." He went silent a moment, but all he got was the hum of a passing vehicle below.

Fabian resisted the urge to shake his head. Victor was obviously still angry. Why is he here then? Maybe it was to remind him of how much he missed their talks, and he did. The six years of adjusting had been difficult, and there was not anyone Fabian could talk to about the transition, speaking to humans on the subject was forbidden.

Even without a human's vastly flawed concept of time, it seemed longer than seven years since his dislike of humans once mirrored Victor's—since he had also disliked the "lesser beings" that God loved so much—.

Fabian spoke slowly, "Victor, we were so wrong about them. I understand that now. Yes, they are capable of great cruelties, but we'd only halfheartedly considered what their lives are like. The dark forces torment them day and night without rest, and they must live in this vastly polluted environment." His jaw tightened. "You and I considered them a pampered ilk, lacking restraint and of low conscience, but we were the spoiled ones. Like spoiled rich kids, we criticized them without understanding their circumstances."

"So you think differing circumstance warrants His favor for them over us?"

Fabian's head turned to the far end of the railing were stood a six-foot-three angel in a flowing, light brown robe. He had broad, off-white wings that would cover the full length of the balcony if he stretched. The angel's hair was white and flowed down between the arches of his wings to well past his waist.

Fabian smiled and raised his arms for a hug but lowered them after reading Victor's expression. "You still believe that?" Fabian asked. "We were wrong, Victor. He loves us too, but his love for us is different, not less. The love a parent has for each child is expressed according to the child."

Victor was a statue; only his mouth moved. "Therefore you turned your back on your closest siblings to mimic another." Victor was looking out into the city, not bothering to make eye contact. He had a casual attitude, as if time and the world around him did not matter. "Is that why you chose to become a descender?"

The muscles in Fabian's jaw flexed as he slowly shook his head at the term. "That was not the reason I chose to be human, Victor."

"Was it not? Then was it for their savage ways? Had you forgotten the endless evils we have seen them commit?"

Fabian walked closer to him. "No. I learned to believe in their potential from watching her."

Victor's upper lip curled. "From the woman? She is no different. She'd toss her nobility, given the right conditions, like the others."

Fabian shook his head. "Must you always judge them so harshly? What about the ones who remained committed during their struggle?"

"A fleeting few at best," Victor snapped.

Fabian leaned his head closer to Victor. "It's those few that I based my decision on. Maybe the Father does, too."

Victor turned to him. "You view your decision to become human as a moment of clarity, but it was not. Only a fool chooses to be less than superior. Soon you will realize your mistake." He finally turned and looked at Fabian with cold, blue eyes. "As yet brother you have only experienced their pleasures firsthand, but soon you shall experience their evils as well."

Fabian's brow creased. "What do you mean? Is my family in danger Victor?"

Victor turned a nonchalant gaze back to the city. "You have indeed lost your virtue, brother. Can you not see the signs? Can you only see that glimmer of light and not the vast darkness around it? They have betrayed you, and now they intend to seek forbidden knowledge once again." He pointed out into the city, "They come for thee."

Fabian felt his legs weaken and a cold shiver go down his spine. Memory serving, he felt fortunate he was not just human. He and placed a hand on Victor's shoulder and closed his eyes.

Almost immediately a two-dimensional, smoke-haze of a vision appeared in Fabian's mind. Its gray, outer area resembled a street with adorning cars, pedestrians and sidewalks. But it was the beastly appearances of three darker images sprinting past the others like ghosts that quickly got Fabian's attention.

The vision was blurred but the fanged and clawed outline of the images left him with no doubt as to their identity.

"Demons," Fabian gasped pulling away from Victor's shoulder. "Help us, Victor! Don't let them hurt my family."

Victor eyes narrowed. "You wanted to be human. Suffering, pain, death. Such is their life." In a blink, he disappeared leaving Fabian alone and near trembling as he stared at the railing.

Fabian swallowed hard, but it did not help the sudden dryness of his throat, at the revelation that his brother had left him there for certain death, a fact that proved just how gravely he had underestimated Victor's feelings. But now it was clear. His brother did not love him anymore.

He hurried back through the balcony door and called out to Heather. "Baby, get up! Baby, come on, you've got to get up!" Reaching the bed, he shook Heather from her sleep

"What's wrong?" Heather asked, squinting and rubbing an eye.

Fabian's words ran together as he urged. "Come on, you must take Gallois to the monastery. Trouble's coming!" He went to a nearby dresser and began stuffing clothes into a large suitcase.

Heather sat up in the bed. "Trouble? Fabian, what's going on?"

Fabian shoved another handful of clothes into the suitcase as Heather noticed the shotgun resting on the sliding door. "Just trust me. You've got to take Gallois and leave."

She tore her eyes from the shotgun. "Fabian, you're scaring me. What's wrong?" She got out of bed, covering her pink and gray pajamas with a navy blue robe.

Fabian dropped what he was doing, and as gently as his panicked nerves would allow, pulled her into his arms. "Someone's coming here, and they mean us harm. You have to take Gallois and leave."

Heather's brown eyes widened with fear. "We should call the police!" she blurted, reaching for the phone. Fabian grabbed her hand. "No. They won't be able help us—It's them."

Heather started to speak but then turned and hurried down the hall. Fabian finished packing the suitcase. He heard a distant screeching noise a hideous sound, like an enraged animal.

"Heather, hurry!" he called.

She came down the hall holding Gallois wrapped in a bed sheet. Fabian strode across the living room and opened the door as Heather reached him.

She walked out the door but stopped, noticing her husband was not following.

"What are you doing? Come on."

Fabian held out the suitcase. "I can't. If I stay, you'll be safe."

"No! No, Fabian. You're coming with us!" She grabbed his arm, but he pulled away.

"It's too late for that. They're close. If I go, they will find us. This is the way it has to be."

Tears began to fill her eyes, Fabian eyes swelled as well. He had known this day would come when he first revealed himself to her. He had tried to pretend they had a chance, but the truth was always there, lurking behind every smile and pleasant moment they shared. He knew she was as worried as he was, though he had never let her dwell on it. He was the optimistic one after all, true to his original self. Now all pretending was ended. All they could do now was try to protect their child from the horrors of their naïve dream. Heather stuttered some words but they were overwhelmed with emotion.

Fabian gently placed a hand on the side of her face and held her gaze with his own. "Every moment with you has been worth it." She pressed her face into the palm of his hand as he rubbed her cheek. He pulled the blanket away from his son's head.

"The fever has broken," Heather said, widening her arms. She tried to wake Gallois but he was too tired from the three different prescriptions he'd been given earlier. Fabian simply said, "No," as he grabbed her hand, knowing it would be harder for him to let them go if she woke him. He removed the blanket so he could see Gallois's full face, smiled and said he loved him before kissing him on the forehead and replacing the blanket.

He flinched as the screeching sounded again. It sounded closer this time but he knew his wife could not hear it.

"You got to go!" he told her. "Now!" They kissed hard and said, "I love you," at the same time and then Fabian wearily pushed them away and watched as Heather ran down the hallway to vanish down a flight of stairs.

Fabian watched the staircase until he could no longer hear her footsteps before turning back inside the apartment. He eased the door and could hardly bring himself to remove his hand from the doorknob. His chest was heavy, and tightness gripped his throat.

As he moved from the door, he noticed Gallois's favorite toy truck resting on the couch, Heather's coffee cup nearby. He remembered watching Heather tickle Gallois in the same spot. The memory of their smiles and Gallois's light laughter brought him to tears.

"Every moment was worth it," he said again.

After a few seconds, he wiped away his tears and looked back at the couch, or rather to the large wooden crucifix that hung above it. He stared at it and considered everything that it signified to him and found a comfort that quickly turned to resilience.

"I will not go easily."

He hurried back to the bedroom. Kneeling down and at the foot of the bed he reached under it and pulled out an old brown chest. "And some of you are going with me."

He pulled back the lid, revealing a tarnished Gladius styled sword made of gold. The pommel of the sword was engraved with a crucifix. The knot was of red leather followed by a rounded cross and rain-guard. The tapered, double-edged was over two feet long and four centimeters wide. He took hold of the pommel, and a thin stream of golden light trailed down the sword, leaving behind a spotless shine. He lifted the weapon from the chest effortlessly as if it were made of steel and walked back to the living room, grabbing a chair on the way. He placed the chair in the middle of the living room and sat down. The screeches sounded again, even more loudly. Whatever it was, it would be there soon.

He sat motionless, realizing he was not scared. Most descenders did not fear death. Why should they? Becoming human did not affect their sense of morality, so after death they knew where they were going. He had figured if there were anything to fear it was the pain of the actual dying. He hoped it would pass quickly.

He looked into the eyes of the round-faced, wooly-haired man staring back at him in the luster of the sword. *How different I have become. As an angel I spent an eternity in complete logic, but in total confusion about the ways of man.*

A vision of Heather flashed through his mind.

When I first saw her she was only twelve years old. Her life was filled with misery. Her father, a holy man, abandoned left her with a drug addicted mother and drug dealer boyfriend who beat her so bad she lost partial hearing in her right ear. Then she was in and out of foster homes, each occupied by people who only cared about receiving the state check.

Through all that, she never held any animosity towards any of them. I saw many people go through less and turn out to be the most evil and hate-ridden of adults. She never lost her compassion for others or her faith in God. From the first time I spoke with her, I knew to be with her was worth giving up my life as an angel. I wish I could stay with her and watch our son grow up. She will take care of him.

He slowly parried the sword. *Who'd be foolish enough to tell someone about me? Only a few know about me: Father Jacob, Heather, select few members of the Vatican.*

His thoughts were interrupted by the fluttering of the lamps. Cold crept down his spine again as an array of muffled, beastly howls sounded from his bedroom. He rose slowly from the chair, and raised the sword as he stared down the hallway. He flinched when he heard something scampering outside the living room window. Various muffled growls began to vibrate the walls that grew in intensity.

Fabian assumed a fierce stance with the sword firmly high in one hand. "Your will be done," he whispered.

~>≡◎ ◎≡<~

Heather's taxi stopped in front of Father Jacob's chapel, a stone nineteenth century-Italian baroque with a limestone façade, rich in decoration amid four Corinthian columns with designs etch within the smaller pediments, carved with scroll motifs.

Standing at fifty feet were twin towers flanking a 150-foot central dome. Heather reached the large solid oak front door with Gallois on her arm. She banged on the door and yelled for Father Jacob as the taxi drove away. Her heart was pounding so hard she could hear nothing else. Just get inside and he'll be safe! Fabian! Finally the door crept open.

"Heather?" questioned an elderly priest, squinting through thick bifocals from the other side of the cracked door. "Come in, child. What are you doing out this hour?"

Heather dragged the suitcase just inside the door. "Please! I need to speak with Father Jacob! Fabian needs help!"

The elderly priest's confused expression faded.

"Fabian? Yes, I'll get him right away." He turned and began making his way down a hallway lit by light coming from a room that must have been where he was sleeping.

Heather checked on Gallois underneath the red glow of the French stained glass depicting a guardian angel with a demon underfoot. He had woken crying halfway through the ride over. She sat down on a pew and propped Gallois up in her arms. He was sleeping now with tear stains marking his cheeks. Footsteps were approaching that became louder as shadows lined the wall. Father Jacob accompanied to her amazement by six uniformed men caring assault weapons.

"Heather, where is he?" Father Jacob asked, adjusting his night robe around his pudgy body.

"At our apartment."

Father Jacob looked over his shoulder and nodded at the six soldiers. They hurried out the door.

He leaned down and got a closer look at Gallois. "Are you two all right?"

"Yes. Fabian. Father, what's going on?" Heather answered, leaning forward and causing Gallois to awaken. The toddler began to cry, his voice was weak and dry.

The priest reached for Heather's arm. "Come. Let's see after the child. My men will contact us soon."

⤙▬▬◉ ◉▬▬⤚

"We're here!" the driver of the van yelled back to the men. Ramiro nodded and cocked his weapon. The other five men did the same as the van came to an abrupt stop in front of Fabian's apartment building. The van door slid open and the men quickly moved out. Their army boots and weapons made a busy sound as they moved to the building's entrance. A large gathering of homeless men watched with tempered scowls as a soldier tampered with the entrance door and the soldiers ran into the building.

The soldiers entered the lobby of the building, a broad rectangular area with brown and black carpet, decorative tan wallpaper and Egyptian-themed decor. Twenty feet above them was the first of many levels of brass, railings through which they could see rows of black doors with brown numberings.

"Move!" Ramiro yelled as they entered an elevator. "Tenth floor!"

As the elevator ascended, the soldiers gripped their weapons with eager anticipation. With a chime the elevator door opened on the tenth floor. The small unit swiftly made their way down the hall. In seconds they stood at- the- ready before a door marked with a number 16. Two soldiers posted up on both sides of the door. The larger of the two soldiers standing to the right knocked and called out for Fabian, but there was no answer.

Ramiro gestured, and the soldier on the left kicked open the door with his thick legs. The soldiers charged into the apartment with their guns held at the ready and were immediately caught off guard by the nearly suffocating smell of sulfur. Each man coughed and wretched, but they soon regained focus and began to search at Ramiro's hand gestures.

The apartment was without power and dark as a cave. The soldiers switched on the flashlights strapped to their guns and entered a wrecked area that looked as though it used to be a living room. Every piece of furniture was either shattered or broken and lay on its side among splinters of wood and plaster.

Ramiro studied the destruction as the other soldiers systematically checked the other rooms. Seconds later a short, red-headed soldier approached.

"What you got, Archie?" Ramiro asked.

"The rooms are clear, sir."

Ramiro lowered his weapon. "Do they look as bad as this one?"

"No, sir."

Ramiro continued studying the room. "It all went down here. He knew they were coming. They came in and took him." He looked to the four soldiers standing behind Archie. "Look around. We need to know which group took him."

Archie wiped sweat from his brow. "What happened here, sir?"

Ramiro stared at the shattered windows and the broken and splintered wall space around them. They appeared to have exploded, but the deep gashes in close proximity told a different story. He could see the brick of the foundation through them, bringing on an awareness that slithered icily down his spine.

One of his men checked for rappel ropes or some other means by which someone of this world would surprise an unsuspecting target.

But the soldier would not find any because what had come for Fabian this night was not human. Ramiro decided against telling them what he knew. He did not want to panic them, and there was still a slim chance that they could leave the building without incident. "They came in through the windows," he said instead. "He tried to fight them." Ramiro's hand tightened on his gun while he calmly looked in the direction of the front door.

"They?" Archie asked with raised eyebrows.

Ramiro read Archie's expression. Always the quick thinker, Archie had already arrived at the same conclusion. "The Aggressor," Ramiro blurted to stop Archie from saying the word given to the evil their theologians told them would accompany an unusual smell of sulfur. "Let's not jump to conclusions. We need all of the details first." He rubbed his nose, wishing he had a facemask to guard against the stench.

"Sir! I think we've found him!" a soldier shouted.

Ramiro and Archie walked over to where the other soldiers had gathered. At their feet was a singed hand sticking-out from beneath an overturned couch. One of the soldiers kicked the couch away, revealing a severely burnt body. It was a man's body, the flesh completely burned away to reveal scorched muscle and bone drawn up in a fetal position like the remains of a vampire exposed to sunlight. There wasn't anything vampiric about its exposed teeth, however it had been human.

"The bastards set him on fire," Archie said, shocked and repulsed.

"No, that's not him. I wish it were." Ramiro said, to everyone's bewilderment except Archie when he noticed that no flammable material had been used and only the body was burnt despite the carpet and couch. He moved to turn away, when something beneath the corpse partly covered by pieces of singed flesh caught his eye. He used the barrel of his weapon to lift the remains to reveal a golden sword partially covered with ash.

He pulled it from the corpse's rib-cage and held it up to study. It gleamed as he turned it. The men in the unit looked on.

"Nice craftsmanship," Archie said.

"You have no idea," Ramiro said, wiping ash from the sword. "That looks like real gold. They just left it behind?"

Ramiro did not answer; he was past being ready to leave the apartment. His shoulder radio crackled with static and his driver's voice sounded then cut-out. Ramiro grabbed the receiver.

"Eric," he said. "Eric, come in," He paused, hearing nothing but static. "Shit! We're going to need another way out of here. Archie call it in! Tell them we need a helicopter on the roof of this building, now!"

Ramiro headed for the front door with the men following close behind, their guns held ready. He looked around the door and down the hallway. There was no one in sight. They poured into the hallway, heading back to the elevator.

"Hold!" Ramiro said with a clenched fist in the air. One of the homeless men came staggering out of the elevator. "Sir, we're going to have to ask you to step aside!"

The man did not answer. Shuffling toward the unit with his head hung low and bobbing with every step as if he were walking in his sleep.

One of the soldiers whispered to Ramiro, "Sir. It's just some homeless guy."

"No, it's not," Ramiro snapped. "No one fires until I say." He aimed his weapon at the man's leg and fired a single shot. The beggar did not miss a step as the bullet ripped through cloth and leg before splintering in the wood behind him. Ramiro fired another round this time at the beggar's thigh. The beggar stopped as blood trailed down his leg. He slowly raised his head, revealing a pair of dilated, blood shot eyes that made the other soldiers raise their guns. A beastly growl rolled up from the beggar's chest, vibrating the building walls before the man slumped over on all fours like a dog and charged at the group. "Fire!" Ramiro yelled. The sounds of gunfire echoed off the walls.

The man shook violently from the force of the bullets tarring through his face and torso in a bloody mess of skin, blood, and bone. He was within five feet of the group before he finally fell to the floor and lay still in an expanding pool of blood.

After the commotion a few apartment tenants wearily poked their heads from the cracked doors of their homes. The soldiers warned them to go back inside as Ramiro stared at the body. Archie cautiously started for the body to check if it were dead. Ramiro grabbed his arm. "No! Leave it." He waved to the group. "Back up. We'll take the stairs. Let's go! Move!"

The unit backed up and headed for a stairwell on the other end of the hallway. One of the soldiers glanced over the railing and saw that the homeless men had been outside were now hovering in the lobby below. One of them looked up, met the soldier's eyes, and roared hideously, gaining the attention of the others who also began roaring and growling. Without warning, they began climbing up the railings like angry gorillas.

"Sir! Sir, look!" the soldier called.

Ramiro and the other men looked down and were transfixed.

"Go! Go!" Ramiro yelled, pushing some of the soldiers into movement. They quickly scrambled down the hall and got to the stairs.

The men-like creatures were already trailing close behind them. One was steadying itself after having jumped over the railing onto their floor.

"Keep moving!" Ramiro commanded as they burst through the stairwell doors and began mounting the steps with the creatures bustling after them.

Two men in the rear fell behind as they fired at the creatures. The sounds of gunfire were deafening in the confined space of the stairwell as bullets broke concrete and ricocheted off of the metal rails. The creatures were getting closer with every level they passed.

The unit was nearly falling over each other but they kept moving. Every man was breathing heavily and sweating. Ramiro looked up the stairwell as he fired a round at the face of one of the creatures. He could see that they were almost at the roof but it was not soon enough for Archie, who had just gotten pulled into the crowd of creatures and frenzied upon in an assault of savage blows that splattered his blood on the stairwell walls.

"No! He's gone! Keep moving!" a soldier shouted, pulling on a colleague spellbound by the savagery. Finally they reached the door to the roof. Three soldiers held the door as one quickly emptied his weapon and used it to barricade the door. The creatures rained blows on the barrier. It would not hold for long.

The faint hum of the helicopter came from overhead as it descended toward them. Once it landed the unit boarded quickly.

"Lift off!" Ramiro yelled.

They quickly ascended with the sound of the propellers roaring in their ears and air rushing around them. Each exhausted man sat motionless, watching the barricaded door slowly fade from sight. As the helicopter sped through the air, the men stared of into space with dismay.

Ramiro looked them over. To a man they were stunned and terrified. He searched for encouraging words although he knew nothing could change the way they felt. "You all handled yourselves well back there. I'm proud of you!" A few of the men nodded, barely acknowledging the compliment.

"Sir, what were those things?" asked one soldier.

"Demons. And they're early."

Father Jacob was standing at his office window when Ramiro entered.

"There was no sign of him. They must have taken him," Ramiro said. Father Jacob nodded with a sigh before limping toward the sofa. "And there's something else. We were attacked by possessed men, at least thirty of them."

Father Jacob stopped short and looked at him curiously. "Possessed? Are you sure?"

"Yes, those things were definitely not human. They had blood in their eyes and their pupils were dilated."

Father Jacob grunted as he sat his plump frame down on a soft leather sofa, forcing air from the cushions. He slowly rubbed a small crucifix that hung from his neck. "Demon-possessed people of that magnitude shouldn't happen for centuries."

"Fabian killed one of them. The body was burnt beyond recognition."

Father Jacob tapped on a large leather-bound book resting beside him. "Scripture tells us that once a demon has used up the person's life force, the demon becomes weak and eventually leaves the body burning like the soul of its owner in hell. There's only one way demons can exist in this era. Something has come from the other side." He rubbed his face wearily. "I have no doubt the Nesphar is involved in some way, but how?" He paused. "How are the men?"

"I lost two, Archie and Hill."

Grief shadowed Father Jacob's face. I need to notify the Vatican and see what they make of this. Those men attacked you directly so they are being controlled by someone. And they know who we are. For now I'll have our men in the police department handle this. They arrived at the apartment shortly after you left."

"What about Hill's and Archie's bodies?"

"I will have them sent here. The police will find a suitable explanation for the press. Go get some rest. I fear things are going to get worse."

Ramiro picked up Father Jacob's walking cane and brought it to him. "I'll see you in the morning, Father." He closed the door on his way out.

Father Jacob glanced at the phone sitting on the desk then removed his glasses and rubbed his eyes. Conversations with the Vatican were always drawn out, followed by a slow response time to anything he asked for. It was going to be hard enough to sleep. Nagging questions filled his mind, and, worse, he had to tell Heather that Fabian was gone.

He had no doubt the Nesphar had taken him. Finding Fabian would be nearly impossible. His hands trembled as he clutched at his robe and turned off the office light before walking the cold hallway to Heather's room. He turned to marvel the stained windows depicting the Holy Communion. They always renewed his faith which was why his chose his current office space over the former Father's office.

He had spent his whole life fighting the Nesphar and satanic cults like it. He had seen many evil things, both natural and supernatural. The Vatican had prepared him for the time of the Apocalypse. He had seen the devil's work through exorcisms, and he knew that demons were very real. He had an aching limp to prove it.

But this situation had elements that he had not anticipated. Demonic forces were being used directly, not sporadically. How can this be? Why did they come after Fabian? How did they find out about him?

He tried to clear his mind and concentrate on what he would say to Heather. He arrived at the door of her room, dreading what lay ahead. He would do all he could to be there for her, to protect her and the child. Fabian had given his life for their safety and trusted him with protecting them.

He knocked. "It's Father Jacob."

Heather opened the door. With red and swollen eyes she looked past him and down the hallway.

"I'm sorry, my child. They took him."

Heathers screamed, collapsing into Father Jacobs's arms too suddenly for him react. She fell to her knees and wrapped her arms around his waist so tightly it hurt. All he could do was drape his arms over her as she cried.

"You're not alone," he said. "We will look for him until he is found. We won't give up."

She didn't seem to hear him. There in the doorway, he held her until her grip loosened and her body went limp with fatigue.

"Come now, try to rest," he said, helping her to her feet before guiding her to a bed across the room.

Tears spilled from her closed eyes as her head dropped onto the pillow, her lips moved as she murmured words he could not make out. Her voice was weak. She was exhausted and would soon be asleep whether she wanted it or not.

He pulled the covers up to her chest and sat at her side until he was sure she was asleep. Then he walked over to a small bed nearby where Gallois lay.

He looked down to find the child tossing in his sleep; probably having a bad dream. Father Jacob gently rubbed his forehead and a moment later Gallois relaxed.

"This is your home now," he whispered. "You will be safe here. I won't let anything happen to you or your mother. I don't know why they came for Fabian but they won't touch you."

Chapter 2

WHOOSH!

Ramiro's fist sailed through the air right where Gallois's face had been a second ago. Slow and predictable Gallois, thought, glancing across the room at his laptop resting on his bed. He was not sure if he had turned it off. He sidestepped, blocked a front kick, and noticed a large smudge on the glass wall enclosing his chamber, he would be sure to wipe it afterwards. Otherwise his mother would definitely notice and he would have to spend another fifteen minutes re-cleaning the entire wall.

He dodged another fist then a foot as he surveyed the rest of his glass then gave a quick glance at his bedroom area on the other side of the room where the glass ended and wood began before giving Ramiro his full attention. It was getting harder for him to pretend these training sessions were a challenge, but he had been told he had to for reasons he never truly agreed with. His mother's words were stuck in his head: Baby, no one is that fast or nearly that strong. People won't understand.

And people feared what they did not understand. So Gallois did as he was told as he always had, always the good her good son besides the last thing he wanted to do was hurt someone.

Gallois faked fatigue as he watched sweat streamed down Ramiro's face and drip past his heaving chest and lowered lead hand. He trailed his eyes from Ramiro's fist and face to telegraph an opening. Ramiro heeded the cue and raised his arm as Gallois watched Lisa, Ramiro's twenty-one-year-old daughter's limber body, circle around him with her long black ponytail dancing at her back.

"He's playing with us, Dad." Lisa said. She flashed a wicked smile. "Weapons?"

Ramiro nodded. "Yeah, weapons. Let's even this out."

Their footsteps sounded softly on the black mat as they ran over and grabbed bo-staffs from a nearby wall. Gallois readied himself. He was lithe and muscular and stood-five-foot-eight. Lisa and Ramiro maneuvered around him. After a few parries they attacked quickly. With a combination of dodges and backflips, Gallois evaded their strikes with masked ease. Ramiro and Lisa pressed their attack harder, moving methodically, trying to corner Gallois. They eventually managed to corner him where the glass enclosing the chamber met wood.

Gallois took a quick backwards glance as he realized the loss of space. His opponents came to a stop when he had no room left.

During the momentary pause, Gallois watched as Lisa glare narrowed more and Ramiro's chest heaved as sweat dripped from his chin.

Without warning, they swung their staffs high and low. Gallois responded by using the wall to back flip over Ramiro's six-three frame. When Gallois landed he was five feet from Ramiro. In one motion Gallois stripped Ramiro's staff from him and used it to sweep his legs from underneath him. Lisa came charging up from behind, swinging her staff with a loud cry.

The loud crack of wood against wood echoed of the thick ceiling beams as Gallois swung around blocked the strike. He and Lisa dueled briefly until Gallois caused one of Lisa's hands to lose grip of her staff and sent her to the mat with a leg sweep. She landed with a hard thud as her staff rolled free.

She and Ramiro lay on the mat, breathing heavily. Gallois crouched down next to them, showing no signs of fatigue.

"We almost got you that time," Lisa said, still gasping.

Ramiro chocked on a laugh. "When do you mean, just before we hit the mat? I think he's getting faster."

Gallois looked away as he smiled in his usual way which they had always taken as shyness but it was really a habit formed by the shame he felt whenever they would praise him, not knowing he was not normal.

Lisa exhaled loudly. "I miss the days when I could hit him. He's only fifteen and already like a master."

"He's come a long way since then," Ramiro said. "But remember, you two, this is only practice. In a real fight make sure your assailant doesn't get back up. You only have one life. Guard it well."

Lisa and Gallois shared a smile. "How can he forget Dad? You say it every practice."

"Ok, smarty-pants, what else do I say almost every practice, hum?"

Lisa smiled coyly. "What?"

Ramiro returned her smile. "You know what. How did Gallois beat you?"

Lisa rubbed her chin. "Let's see, Sifu. He beat me by having the speed of a freak."

Ramiro shook his head. "Wrong. Gallois help her out."

"You fought the guard again," Gallois murmured.

Ramiro pointed. "That's right Lizzy. You fought the guard during the last exchange. That's why you're on your ass now. When Gallois blocked you high, you tried to force your stick through it, which allowed him to use your energy against you and strip your weapon." He raised his index finger. "So I say again, if your opponent blocks you, go to another area of attack or—"

"Use the block to your advantage," Lisa finished. "It's hard to remember that stuff during the fight."

"That's the purpose of training. You try to remember now, so you won't have to later, even if it means you have to lose."

Gallois looked at Lisa, knowing the next words out her mouth would be in agreement but also that she would not mean it. She hated to lose, she always had. If someone beat her three consecutive times at any anything she would quit.

Before Lisa could speak her empty words, they heard the electronic key lock of Gallois's chamber chime, and a figure stepped out of a sanitizing mist. It was Malcolm Elton, Lisa's boyfriend of two years and sergeant under Ramiro's command.

"Seven-thirty already?" Ramiro asked, glancing over at a clock on the wall.

Lisa scoffed then hurried to her duffle bag resting near the training mat. "Dad, tell him I'll be out in a minute," Lisa grabbed the bag and her red sundress beside it. She hurried into a locker room just beyond Gallois's small indoor pool. She would return in ten minutes with damp skin wearing the dress and high heels. She had mastered the art of getting dressed in a hurry mostly because she had radiant skin and high cheek bones that did not need makeup.

"Late as usual. Malcolm should be used to it by now," Ramiro said.

Malcolm approached Gallois and Ramiro with a broad smile. "Hello, Mr. Vasquez, Gallois. How's training going?"

Ramiro look at Gallois with a quick smile. "Fine, Malcolm. She'll be out soon."

Gallois knew Malcolm well enough to know he was irritated because Lisa wasn't ready when he arrived. As a soldier Malcolm had the typical stern and orderly way about him, much like Ramiro. Gallois assumed the similarity was why Lisa liked him. She had talked constantly about him before Gallois had even met him. All Gallois kept hearing was how cute and smart some un-named guy was. The absence of a name had suggested to Gallois the guy was one of Ramiro's soldiers. Surprisingly, when Ramiro learned of their relationship he did not seem to object to it.

"So where are you two off to tonight?" Ramiro asked.

"We're planning to go to a Knicks game. They're playing the Lakers."

Excitement showed on Ramiro's face, but Gallois knew he'd never followed basketball. He and Gallois preferred combative spots like boxing. "Oh, that'll be a good one. I didn't know Lisa liked basketball."

"She doesn't. I'm hoping that seeing a live game will get her into it. Hey, why don't you come with us?"

Ramiro raised his palms. "No, no, I don't want to be a third wheel. Besides, I'm going to need some ice packs and a rest after training with Gallois." He grabbed at Gallois' shoulder, and Gallois smiled shyly.

Malcolm smiled. "Lisa told me he's gotten really good."

Ramiro turned and walked to a towel rack. "I'd say better than good. He's a bit of a prodigy. I've never seen anyone learn so fast."

As Ramiro walked away, Gallois felt the usual heat of anger from Malcolm whenever Ramiro turned his back. When Gallois's gaze returned to Malcolm, he found him mouthing fuck you with a crooked smile. Gallois did not know what he'd done to make Malcolm hate him so much or why he always played this game. It really made him angry but he did not want to make it worse. And as much as he resisted the thought, he hoped they could get past it and become friends.

Malcolm's demeanor shifted back to pleasantries when Ramiro turned around. "Really? The best you've trained?" Malcolm asked, staring blankly at Gallois before rolling his eyes. "That's saying a lot, after all the students you've had, myself included. You know, you should put him in the unit."

The words crushed Gallois, and brought the sting of tears to his eyes but he would not give Malcolm the satisfaction of knowing it. Lisa must have told him that was Gallois wanted most, and Malcolm knew that it would not ever happen and why.

"I'm giving it serious thought," Ramiro responded quickly as he returned, wiping his neck with a damp towel.

Father Jacob led everyone to believe Gallois had photophobia and an immune system disease, which were the reasons for the tinted goggles and living in the chamber. But the truth was that only once in his life had Gallois ever been ill. The chamber and goggles were ways to hide Gallois's abnormality and keep the Nesphar from getting to him. No one was allowed to see Gallois without Father Jacob's say-so.

Fifteen torturous minutes passed as Malcolm and Ramiro talked while waiting for Lisa, and Gallois was angry during all of them. Ramiro tried to include him in the conversations, but with Lisa and Ramiro being the only two people with whom he usually interacted with, he did not have the social skills or the desire to converse with Malcolm.

"I'm ready," Lisa said, coming from the locker room carrying the duffle bag.

Gallois breathed a quiet sigh of relief.

Malcolm looked at his watch. "Great. We'd better get going. We'll be late."

"See you two later," Lisa said as she breezed by and grabbed Malcolm's arm.

Gallois stood there and watched as Ramiro waved goodbye to the pair then turned to him, saying,

"Okay, I think I'm ready. Do you want to practice a little longer?" He picked up Lisa's bo-staff and placed it back on the wall.

Gallois nodded and adjusted his navy blue workout gloves before picking up Ramiro's bo.

Gallois faked a smile as Ramiro returned, trying to mask the lingering sadness he felt from Malcolm's comment. Unfortunately for him, Ramiro had a way of just knowing how he felt. Gallois hoped he would not try to talk about it again. It hurt Gallois to hear Ramiro's kind words knowing he was comforting with a lie. Instead he hoped for the usual redirecting of his attention, which Gallois was more than happy to help along.

"Your weapon, sir," he said in a playful tone with an outstretched arm.

Ramiro took the staff from him and tried a surprise lunged, thrusting the staff at Gallois. Gallois countered the move, taking the staff from his hands and bringing its tip just inches from Ramiro's chest. Ramiro froze. Gallois held the staff out to him again.

"Right," Ramiro said with a laugh.

Gallois smiled.

--◦▬◉ ◉▬◦--

Heather stepped into her son's chamber, quietly taking a nervous breath as the electronic door locked behind her. She tightened her grip on the lid of her food tray and waited for the sanitizing mist to flush over her body. As the mist cleared, she closed her eyes, hoping the act she was about to put on would be convincing enough to fool her curious child. Taking a few steps, she spotted Gallois sitting at the oak dining table that used to furnish their apartment.

She had managed to fit nearly every expensive piece of furniture she and Fabian owned into the chamber, from the brown leather sofa and loveseat that used to be in the living room to the oak bookshelf that had furnished the study. The furnishings did not give the room a homey appearance, but seeing the remembrances of her past life were a comfort and she hoped Gallois too.

Forcing a smile, she carefully approached the dining table and uncovered the tray of food before sliding it in front of Gallois. On the tray were two plates of the usual food groups, but one added meat serving for Gallois. She was worried that he was not getting enough nourishment with all his training. Tonight it was steak, green beans, wheat bread, and a slice of homemade apple pie.

Heather smiled as she sat down at the table. "Hi, honey. I hope you're hungry. I grilled these, and they're pretty big."

"Hi, Mom," Gallois said, removing his gloves and placing them on the table next to the tray.

Heather made herself comfortable in the chair opposite him. "So how was training? Ramiro said you're fighting two peopl—. Honey, take off those goggles. You know I can't talk to you with those things on."

Gallois slowly pulled off the goggles to reveal his brown eyes. "Ramiro said we'll try three tomorrow." He picked up his fork, and one of his mother's eye brows rose.

"Forget something?" she asked.

"Oh, sorry." Gallois lowered his head and blessed his food and then began cutting into the steak.

They ate in silence for several minutes before his mother asked, "You want to watch a movie when you're finished?"

Gallois only shook his head, his mouth full. His mother looked up at the glass ceiling and the small balcony above them.

"Well, it's a beautiful night. You want to look at the stars?"

Gallois looked up from his plate and quickly finished chewing his food. "Something's bothering you. What's wrong, Mom?"

Heather was briefly tongue-tied as she wondering what gave her away.

"Nothing," she said, placing a hand over his. "Everything's fine."

Gallois studied her face as he often did when people spoke to him, a mannerism that reminded her so much of his father.

"Are you sure? Truthfully, nothing's bothering you?"

"—If there were something to worry about I'd tell you," she said.

Gallois placed his other hand on top of hers and she pulled her it away with a disciplining frown. "You know it's not polite to read people's minds without their permission, especially when that person is your mother."

Gallois protested, "I wasn't going to. I just wanted to know if you were telling the truth."

Heather paused before explaining her-self, her faith reminding her how similar withholding information was to a lie. "I didn't want to tell you because I didn't want you to be worried." She exhaled as she clasped her hands together. "But I know you won't rest now until you know." She shot him a scolding look. "Even if you have to wait until I am asleep. So I'll just tell you. Two of the priests went missing, Fathers Harold and Gibbs. Do you remember them? Sorry, of course you do."

Gallois had a photographic memory, which, along with his clairsentience, was one of his "gifts." as Father Jacob called them, one that he had used to help keep untrustworthy priests and nuns from being brought into the monastery.

"How long have they been missing?" Gallois asked.

"It's been four days now. No one's heard from them."

Gallois whispered, "Do they think it's the Nesphar?"

"Yes." She read the look on his face. "Don't worry. You know Ramiro can take care of himself. He has all this time, hasn't he?"

"I know," Gallois said as he looked down at his plate and awkwardly spooned up a few green peas. "He always comes home."

Heather watched him as he chewed the peas at length, knowing he would be very distant until Ramiro had returned safely.

Chapter 3

RAMIRO AND MALCOLM stood before Father Jacob's desk with eager expressions wondering why they had been suddenly called to his office. The priest picked up two folders from his desk and handed one to each of them.

"We have a green light," he said, fidgeting his clasped hands.

"What is this?" Malcolm asked as he flipped back and forth between two black-and-white photos of two three-story buildings.

"It's one of two of the Nesphar's black mass churches here in New York. As you know, the Nesphar usually move around, congregating in secret locations as a way of avoiding detection whenever they conduct some sick ritual that they believe will empower them with attributes from beyond. Well, it seems they're becoming less discreet."

Malcolm looked up from the folder skeptically. "I know these buildings. Their windows are painted black. I thought they weren't leased. How long have you known of this?"

Father Jacob studied the soldier's disapproving stare before answering. "I've only learned of it fifteen minutes ago, but the Vatican apparently has known about it for the past year and a half."

"A year and a half? Really? We've been trying to shut these jerks down, and they keep this from us?"

"I understand your frustration," the older man said to the impatient youth with as much sympathy as he could muster. "The Vatican's been observing these structures for some time, but they didn't have a reason for concern until now. Take a look at the second photo."

Ramiro and Malcolm studied the image of a group of men group of men guiding two blindfolded men into a building.

"These were taken the day Fathers Harold and Gibbs went missing," the priest explained. "There's a good chance that these two men are they. Even if they aren't, it looks as though these two men have been kidnapped."

Malcolm placed the file on Father Jacob's desk. "If we had shut them down already this wouldn't have happened! Now they want us to stop them."

"Satanism isn't a crime," Ramiro said, taking another look at the picture. "This place is located uptown. I'm going to need all my men to take down a place of this size."

Father Jacob nodded. "You have it and anything else you need."

"What about the other structure?" Ramiro asked.

"Both will be assaulted tonight. Everson's unit is already on their way to the location." Father Jacob shifted more of his weight onto his good leg.

"Malcolm, go get the men ready," Ramiro ordered, closing the folder.

The soldier hurried out of the room.

When Malcolm's footsteps faded away, Ramiro laid the folder down on the desk and said, "There's a strong possibility that they know they're being watched. I'm sure they have hidden entrances into this place. Why would they so blatantly show that they have two kidnapped men? It feels like a trap."

"We have an informant inside who says they haven't obtained any weapons."

"An informant?" Ramiro asked with raised brows.

Father Jacob hesitated. "It's Oliver Hess."

Ramiro's mouth dropped open." Hess was the fourth richest person in America and notorious for flaunting his wealth and high opinion of himself. The last person that would come to mind in matters of religious morality.

"Oliver's been undercover now for two years now. The Vatican's not saying, but apparently something changed him."

"Two years?" Ramiro gasped. "They appointed you the position of coordinator for this area and kept you in the dark about this until now?"

Father Jacob lowered his head and shuffled papers on the desk. "On matters such as this, I prefer it because I don't have to worry about their risky actions."

"They know I can't assure his safety." Ramiro said.

"He was aware of the risk." Father Jacob said.

Ramiro nodded slowly then looked back at the file. "I'll need the building's blueprints, and I want to use small explosives."

"Take whatever you need. I want those men, whoever they are, freed and this assemblage stopped."

Ramiro turned to leave. "We'll leave in an hour and enter the building at the same time the other unit enters the other site."

"God be with you," Father Jacob said as the soldier exited.

Chapter 4

HEATHER SAT ON a sofa reading a Christian romance novel. She turned a page, and then looked over to Gallois sitting at a desk in the small reading area. His laptop was in front of him, and the image of a computer game reflected on his goggles as he lazily tapped on the keyboard. She watched for several seconds before realizing he was not playing the game but just pretending he was.

She guessed he was thinking deeply, and she did not need to wonder what he might be thinking about. Despite Father Jacob's efforts to make the room less of a chamber, each year Gallois seemed to outgrow its walls. The past few months she noticed he had lost interest in most things, and he talked less, obvious signs of a discontented child that any good parent would notice.

God! How she wanted more for him! He should not be living like this. He should be in high school, complaining about teachers, asking to go to the mall with friends, and nagging her to teach him to drive.

But she knew, even if he could do those things, her son would not be like most teenagers. Even now he was not concerned with teenage interests. He would rather read than watch television. He admired men like Martin Luther King Jr., and Epictetus. She could not see him imitating some teen heart-throb. As much as she hated to admit it, her son in public school would be the outcast, the poor kid who sat alone at lunchtime. She definitely did not want that; there had to be some better life for him.

She stared at the sad expression on her son's face, and the thought of having failed him took hold of her. Tears stung her eyes as she placed a hand on her stomach where, beneath her blue cotton shirt, the scar tissue of an emergency C-section was still visible. Unbeknownst to Gallois he was her third-born, the only surviving child of quadruplets. She thought about her husband, wishing he were there, and had an idea.

"Gallois, come here."

Her son came over and sat down beside her, asking before she could speak, "Tell me again about my father."

She hesitated, forcing a smile.

"There is something I want to give you." She walked across the room to his bed.

Gallois watched as she opened a secret compartment on his headboard, pulled something out, and returned with something long wrapped in a white cloth.

"I'd planned to give this to you on your eighteenth birth-day," she said. "But now seems like the good time." She pulled away the cloth to reveal a golden sword.

"Wow! That's for me?"

Heather nodded, and Gallois took the sword and turned it slowly. "It's heavy. Where'd you get it?" he asked, running his forefingers down the side of the blade.

Heather fidgeted nervously as she watched him with the sword, not knowing how he was going to take what she had waited years to tell him. She drew in a breath. "I'll try to explain this the best I can. You've read the bible, so you know that Satan and his demons were cast down from Heaven to earth by God. So they are here with us, and since then they have been trying to ruin mankind. There's really only one way he can do this, and that's by our accepting him. I know it's a wonder as to why someone would accept him, but—"

Gallois interrupted. "Genesis, chapter three, verses one through six. He makes us believe that he wants good things for us. He manipulates us like he did with Eve." With his photographic memory he could recall the bible well, but since he knew very little about the real world or the struggles of day-to-day living, it was in some aspects a book of stories to him.

"Well, it's not that simple, Gallois. Life is complicated and the human mind is even more complicated. There have been people who devoted their lives to understanding why we're the way we are and still only come up with theories." She looked at a photo of Gallois and Father Jacob taken five years ago. "Some people are good, like Father Jacob, who care about others and doing good. But you have other people, like the ones we are hiding from, who don't."

"The devil makes them that way?" Gallois asked.

"No. Not always. Some people are evil all on their own."
She leaned forward on the couch, resting her arms on her knees.
"Remember when those soldiers snuck in here four years ago
before the glass wall was built?"

She did not mention that the day had been the anniversary
of Fabian's kidnapping.

Gallois forehead creased. "Yes. One of them called me a
thing."

"Remember how angry you were and how bad you felt after
you'd hurt them? You knew those men just wanted to see who was
living in here, like the others. But that day, you were already angry
and not yourself." She exhaled. "What I'm trying to say is living
is hard. Sometimes we fail to be good people or to do the right
thing. I don't think the devil is the reason for every bad act, but I
do think he exploits our weaknesses for his benefit, regardless of
whether we're trying to be good people or not. Satan is a liar and a
cheat. God knows that, and he's sent angels to protect us."

Gallois stood and parried the sword. "Did Dad practice
martial arts too?"

"Yes he did," she answered with a smile.

Gallois thrust the sword then sliced through the air.
"How come Ramiro never talks about him? Didn't they fight
together?"

Heather took the weapon from him and gestured for him to
sit down as she gently pulled off his goggles. She took a breath
as Gallois sat quietly. "Your father—, he did fight against the
Nesphar. But he wasn't a soldier. He fought with the angels."

Gallois face puzzled.

"Baby, do you know what a Nephilim is?" she asked, knowing that Father Jacob had omitted all information about Nephilims from the electronic bible he had read.

"No," he answered with an unusually confused expression.

She put a hand on his thigh. "Nephilim is what they call someone who is half-angel and half-human. Honey, that's what you are."

Gallois eyes slowly shone golden-yellow as his face turned to stone. He did not move or blink for several seconds. When he finally moved, his head lowered, and he had a faraway gaze.

"Your father was an angel," she went on. "This was the sword he used to fight demons." She placed a hand on his thigh. "I'm telling you this now because I think that you are old enough to understand. And I want you to know why you have to live differently from other people. The Nesphar want to use you to help Satan corrupt the Earth."

Gallois lifted his head. "I would never help them."

"I know," she said softly.

"Is that why they took Dad?"

"Yes. But I know he wouldn't help them either."

"So why did they take him?"

"I don't know, baby, but he let them so they wouldn't hurt us."

Gallois contemplated her words for a while. "I thought angels were different from us. How was I born?"

She put the sword down on her lap. "God gave angels the freedom of choice, just like us. Your father chose to live as a human."

"Why?" he asked.

Her voice cracked. "To be with me."

Gallois began to speak but stopped.

"What is it?" she asked. "Don't be afraid. You can ask me anything. I want you to know everything."

Gallois hesitated again but finally asked, "When an angel becomes human, do the other angels remember him?"

"What do you mean?"

"Are they still friends after that? Do they still know him even though he's human?"

Heather faltered. Fabian never spoke of communicating with the angels.

"I'm sure they do. But your father lost most of the memory of his angelic life."

Gallois looked frustrated. "If the angels knew who he was, why wouldn't they help him the night he was taken?"

Heather looked away, not knowing how to respond to the question she had asked herself a thousand times. "I don't know, baby. There are a lot of things that are not for us to know or understand. We just have to keep believing and endure what comes."

Gallois suddenly grew angry. His expression hardened, and he withdrew from her line of sight. "That's what Father Jacob says when he doesn't have an answer!" His brow furled even more as he yelled out, "I want to know why! Why do we suffer when he has the power to stop it? Why do innocent people die! Why are babies born sick?"

He snatched the sword from his mother's lap and thrust it into his punching bag, puncturing it and causing sand to spill to the floor.

"Gallois!" Heather took the sword before he could strike the bag again and grabbed him by the shirt. "What's gotten into you?"

Gallois tried to withdraw from her hold.

"Hey!" she yelled, tightening her grip. "What is wrong with you?"

Gallois did not answer. He stood there body taut and eyes fiery.

"Maybe I should've waited a little longer," she said.

"Yeah, maybe you should've," Gallois sneered.

Heather glared at him, but she restrained from scolding him. Telling a child that one of his parents had once been an angel was more than a lot to take.

She drew in a breath and exhaled before placing her hands on Gallois's cheeks. "What's wrong? Talk to me. I understand this is a lot, but you needed to know. You have a right to know the truth. I didn't want any secrets between us." She rubbed Gallois' head.

"I saw it," he mumbled.

"Saw what?"

"I saw when they took him." he said.

She chuckled awkwardly. "You couldn't have seen that Gallois, you weren't there." But then she thought of Gallois crying in the taxi on the way to the monastery the night Fabian was abducted. Gallois cried for weeks after that night. She had suspected Fabian and Gallois had some unnatural bond. Gallois would often already be reaching for Fabian just before he turned around to pick him up.

She grabbed Gallois by the arm. "How come you never told me?"

"Because I knew it would upset you."

"Well, you can tell me now," she said. "What happened? Tell me everything." Her grip tightened.

Galois's eyes welled with tears as the words spilled from his mouth. She listened as her son told her how he had seen the torture of his father through his father's eyes. He said he could hear and see everything, including his father's labored breaths as he begged for the demons to finish him. But they would not even when he provoked them. They continued beating him, taking pleasure in screams they thought no one could hear. Gallois said he did not know what blow or bite caused his father's death, but he was certain his father had died because the visions had ended the way they started, with demons looking down upon him before everything turned black.

When Gallois stopped talking, his mother's hands were shaking as she squeezed her crucifix. "Did you see where they took him?"

Gallois suddenly sounded tired. "No. I only saw when they hit him."

"Have you had other visions of him?"

"No."

She looked at his forearm and saw her fingernails had marked his skin. She embraced him. "I'm sorry. And I'm sorry you had to live with that." She lifted his chin in her direction. "You don't have to hide anything from me. It's you and me, remember? It's always been you and me."

Chapter 5

RAMIRO'S TRANSPORT VAN pulled up to the front of a cathedral carrying fifteen of his soldiers. He looked around at the taut faces of his men as they sat wearing black-and-gray camouflage with their assault rifles in their laps. Ramiro got up and crouched in the thin aisle in-between the two rows of soldiers. "OK. We're not sure if this building is hostile, so use caution. And remember, nonlethals only unless fired upon! Stick to the plan of attack. We'll handle only the first two levels. The other group is going around the back from there. They'll make their way to the third and fourth floors. When we have the whole building I'll give further instructions. Let's move!" The soldiers rushed out of the van and gathered at the building's entrance.

A young soldier sat in a surveillance room of the monastery watching television. A nightly news trailer came on. "In tonight's news, the murder rate in America is at an all-time high. American's weigh in on President Randle's crime reduction speech from earlier today. News Nightly, at eleven."

The soldier looked over at the surveillance monitors and noticed three men wearing hooded, black robes standing on the sidewalk in front of the monastery. One of the men looked up toward the camera. The screen crackled then turned to static. He tapped on one of the screens, and then checked the controls.

He picked up a phone. "The cameras went out! No. All of them! Three men came to the entrance, and they went out."

⋯▸▩◉ ◎▩◂⋯

A soldier wearing an ear-piece turned to Lisa as she stood behind him inside the small communications room. He had just informed her that her father and his team just entered the Nesphar's building when the lights in the room began to flicker.

"Silent alarm," said another soldier wearing audio head-phones.

Lisa grabbed a bulletproof vest, radio, and silenced MP gun from a nearby shelf. No sooner than she had done so when three armed soldiers rushed into the room.

"What is it Harper?" she asked.

Harper was a fairly new soldier. He looked far more worried than he should. "We got men at the front entrance. We're going down to check it out. You two keep listening. Father Jacob wants to be notified of what's happening with the two units." He turned to leave the room.

"Harper, I'm coming with you," Lisa said, holstering a pistol.

Harper nodded. "Okay. We're sending a man down. We'll cover him."

With that they stormed out of the room.

⸱⊷⊶⸱

A flash of adrenaline rushed over Gallois. Panicked, he rose from the couch, heart racing, and flushed with beads of sweat. In an instant, he recognized the all-too-familiar signs, but this time they felt more intense than ever before. His heart quickened again when he realized the only logical reason for the increased sensation. The evil that took his father had found him. He ran to his mother who was asleep on the recliner and nearly choked on the words when he shook her awake. "Mom, they've found us! They're here! The demons are here!"

His mother seemed not to need any more clarification than the terror in his eyes. She bolted from the chair and pulled him by the arm. "Where are they? How much time do we have?"

"I'm not sure. They're close."

In seconds, they made their way past the sanitation area to the large main door of the chamber. Heather quickly turned its bank vault-styled lock and shoved it open. They ran across the open foyer to the elevator on the opposite end. As they neared the elevator, Gallois feared the possibility of a demon inside it waiting for them. "You remember what to do if we get separated?" his mother asked as they neared the elevator, perhaps having the same worry.

Before Gallois could answer, a sharp pain spiked behind his eyes, causing him to fall to the floor. When he looked up, expecting to see his mother's face, he saw the end of a row of pews. Confused, he tried to stand up and his hand passed through the armrest as if he were a ghost. Was he dead? Had he been killed and not even felt it? If he had been what was that muffled rhythmic thumping like a heartbeat?

He tried again to stand, having success this time by pushing himself up from the floor. He saw an elderly priest standing with three unusually tall, robed men in the aisle over. He looked the strange figures over carefully and realized they were not men at all. He could feel the evil radiating off them and feared for the life of the old man.

Gallois called out, trying to get their attention. Hopefully the old man would move away. But no matter how loudly Gallois shouted they could not hear him. A door opened behind Gallois, and he saw three armed soldiers sneak into the room. Nervously, he watched as the soldiers took up positions behind pews, knowing that blood was about to be spilled from everyone except the robed creatures. Then Lisa snuck into the room and Gallois's heart sank into his stomach. He yelled as loudly as he could for her to get out of the room, for her to run. But just like the others, she could not hear him. He took a step in her direction, and the vision ended. He found himself back on the foyer floor.

"Are you alright?" his mother asked as she helped him to his feet.

"Mom! Lisa! She's down there! They're going to kill her! We've got to help her!"

They hurried to the elevator, and when they reached it his mother pressed the call button and dropped the hammer on him. "We can't help her now," she said with a somber stare. "We've got to get to the basement. There's a vehicle and a way out."

Gallois looked at her with dismayed as if she were playing some cruel joke on him. She had to be a joking because there was no way his mother would leave Lisa. She loved Lisa. But right now there he could see no concern for Lisa in her eyes, only complete desperation. The birdcage elevator noisily reached their floor and stopped with a noisy rattle of its chain door.

Gallois spoke in a shaky voice. "Mom, I can't leave her—. I can't let her die."

"Gallois, you can't help her now! You know what they do. If you go down there they'll kill both of you! Is that what you want, the two of you dead? Lisa wouldn't want that." She pulled hard on his shirt. "Now, listen to me. Listen to your mother. We have to go!" She slid back the elevator chain door and pulled Gallois inside with her waiting for him to reply.

Gallois felt nauseated as the elevator slowly started to descend and the floor of his chamber began to rise above them. Without warning, Gallois leaped onto the fence, climbed up, and jumped back onto the floor of his chamber before his mother knew what was happening. He could still hear her calling for him as he flung open the door to the stairwell.

⤗▬⊙ ⊙▬⬰

"Can I help you?" asked an elderly priest, as he approached the three men. He coughed and put a hand over his nose as the taller of the men stepped forward and spoke in a deep, raspy, hiss.

"We are here for Father Jacob. Tell him Leba has come for him.

The priest looked them over. Their eyes were covered by their hoods. Only their noses, mouths and boney chins were visible.

"I'm sorry," the priest said. "But he's unavailable. Can I be. . ." He faltered from the sound of throaty growls coming from Leba's comrades.

Leba hissed. "Unavailable? That can't be." He pulled away his hood, revealing his curse, gaunt face. He wore black sunglasses that stood out against, his sweaty, chalk-white skin.

Leba smiled wickedly, showing jagged front teeth. He sniffed the air like an animal. "Cause I can smell his stench!" He grabbed the old priest by the neck. "And the stench of the pathetic sheep around us!" He looked to his left at Lisa hiding behind a pew.

"Bring the priest to me!"

Lisa came out of hiding with the laser-sight of her gun aimed at Leba's chest. "Like the man said, he's unavailable. I suggest you let him go and leave! Now!" She moved her aim to his head.

Leba's black shades turned on her. "You lump of flesh. I am death!" He looked at his associates. "Bleed them!" With a sickening, snap he broke the old priest's neck and flung his lifeless body thirty feet into the pews.

Lisa was still looking at the dead priest's feet dangling over the backrest of the pew when the sounds of the soldiers' guns jolted her. She watched as bullets tore through the robes of Leba's comrades, revealing them for the frightening creatures that they were: bulky, beady-eyed, fanged beasts with long limbs and claws.

With their mouths agape and roaring defiantly at the soldiers' efforts, they shielded Leba from harm and did not move on the soldiers until they went to reload. Then they charged at the soldiers with unnatural speed as Leba walked in Lisa's direction. Lisa fired her weapon at Leba until her gun went empty, but Leba remained standing. He did not even bleed despite the holes in his robe.

"Shit! What the fuck are you?" Lisa yelled as she reloaded her weapon.

Leba quickened his pace, stretching out his arms as though welcoming the bullets.

Lisa heard Harper screaming, but she did not take her eyes off Leba.

As he started running toward her, she fired more rounds. A bullet knocked the sunglasses from his face, revealing a sight that made her scream and drop to her knees. Leba did not have any eyes. In the place where they should have been were two gaping black holes.

She screamed again as the gun fell from her hands. Leba swung at her head. Instinctively, she ducked and just missed being hit, but the second punch landed before she could move to her feet. The force from it put her on her back.

"Lisa!" a soldier cried out as he scrambled to make his way to her. His path was immediately cut off by one of the creatures. He fired his shotgun into its chest only to be grabbed by the neck and have his head pulled from his body.

"Motherfuckers!" the last of the soldiers yelled as he fired his weapon at the creatures.

Lisa moved slowly on the floor. Blood trailed from her forehead and dripped to the floor as her hands searched for her gun. Her hand swept across Leba's foot. She scrambled backwards into the wall, and Leba's massive hands yanked her up by the head. She screamed as she tried to pry his hands away. After a few seconds her body shook and she went still. Leba grabbed her by the throat and growled as he studied her face.

A loud noise diverted his attention to across the room. The other creatures joined his gaze. They began to hissed and growl at the sound of approaching footsteps. Leba dropped Lisa like a ragdoll and looked to the second floor of pews as the footsteps grew louder.

Gallois appeared from the darkness, jumping down to the main floor. He righted himself and looked at the creatures.

Pushing himself up from the floor, the last of soldiers called out to Gallois, screaming for him to run. The soldier stiffened when Gallois turned to him. Gallois had left his goggles in his chamber and his eyes shone their golden yellow in the gloominess of the room.

The sound of Leba's minions growling and hissing brought Gallois's attention back to them. He took small steps toward the culprits, clinching his fists.

The minions advanced but stopped after a quick bark from Leba.

"The time has come half-breed," Leba said. "Soon the Heavens will be in ruin and Satan will claim this world. All mankind therein will suffer unto his will! Commit yourself to him now or suffer with the rest of the brood!"

A tear dropped from Gallois's eye as he glared at Leba. "I'm with them. Like my father."

"Then you will die as he did!"

Gallois's eyes trailed to Lisa lying on the floor behind Leba and his eyes welled with tears. She was not moving. He was too late. He looked back a Leba and the monster grinned at him. Gallois began to breathing heavily as his hands formed into tight fists. He yelled as he began charging at Leba, but the other demons quickly blocked his path and attacked him with quick, powerful strikes.

Gallois ducked under the swinging claw of the closest creature and smashed a hook into its ribs that despite Gallois's smaller stature nearly lifted the beast from the floor. It howled from another blow to its head, and then dropped to the floor as Gallois evaded the snap of the second creature's fangs. He kicked the creature hard between its legs, and it fell over onto the other creature and received a claw to the face and then a shove.

Gallois could still not get more than three steps in Leba's direction before the creatures were back up and on him again. Gallois continued to avoid their attempts. Soon realizing he was more skilled than they were, he delivered flurries of punches that sent the creatures tumbling to the floor. But no matter how hard he hit them, they would not stay down. They were relentless, bounding off pews, trying cheap shots. The creatures circled again as Gallois studied their movements. When they advanced, Gallois tossed one creature head first into a wall, and then, in one motion, he got the other in an arm lock and broke one of its legs. Howling with pain, the creature slumped to the floor.

The other creature came running up from behind. Gallois punched it the throat and broke its arm. The creature swung with its other arm. Gallois broke it and one of its legs. The creature dropped to the ground, screaming and flailing like a wounded animal.

Wasting no more time with them, Gallois scanned the area for Leba and saw him standing at a window. He did not take his eyes off him as he picked up a piece of a broken pew and continued walking in his direction.

Leba flashed a jagged, toothy smile. "You fight in vain, half-breed. This world is already ours!" He threw himself through the window with a crash.

When Gallois reached the window, all he saw was broken glass scattered about the ground. Angry and disappointed, he made his way to Lisa and found that the remaining soldier was already holding her.

"Lisa! Come on, Lisa!" the soldier was urging.

Lisa moved slightly, moaning something incoherent.

Gallois knelt down close to them, startling the soldier. "Is she all right?"

The soldier grabbed his gun from the floor and aimed it at Gallois. "What the hell are you?"

Gallois hesitated looked down the barrel of the gun. "I am her friend." He moved slowly as he crouched and stretched out his arms. "We shouldn't stay here."

Hesitantly, the soldier lowered his weapon and laid Lisa in his arms. "I'll call for help." He looked at the creatures moaning and writhing on the floor. The bloody masses that used to be their eyes were now a grayish black. "What about them?"

Gallois used his clairsentience to look inside of the creatures. Beyond their hideous elongated faces and dilated eyes Gallois could see the thin, shadowy skeletons of their tormented souls imprisoned within.

Their pale faces were fixed in pain.

"They won't bother us now." he said.

Disbelief showed on the soldier's face. "Why not? What's happening to them?"

"I think they're dying," he said as though he were afraid of the words. "You should hurry."

The soldier spoke into his radio.

Gallois looked down at Lisa as the soldier's voice faded away. He brushed hair from her face, noticing for the first time how much her appearance had changed since he had met her years ago. He remembered the day Ramiro introduced him to his talkative daughter. She had been quiet at first as she hid behind her father's legs in a navy-blue dress. When her father left the chamber she turned to him and asked. "Why are you wearing goggles?"

His first words to her had been a lie.

A thin drop of blood trailed from her scalp down the side of her face. He looked at the creatures and dead bodies around him. He made this happen. Men were dead because of him. And he had almost run from it.

He looked back at Lisa. Why should they die because of me? He glared at the demons whose sinister eyes had not turned from his direction. Never again. He would not let anything happen to her or anyone else because of him. This was his problem, his curse, and if the demons were to kill him, he did not want it to happen while he was hiding like a coward.

Tires screeched outside the Chapel. Gallois knew it was no doubt his very angry mother.

The soldier returned. "We need to rendezvous at the hospital. The Vatican has a ward set aside for us."

Gallois nodded as his mother hurried into the church holding a shotgun. "Have they heard from the soldiers?" he asked.

The soldier shook his head wearily. "They lost contact shortly after we came up here."

"With which one?" Gallois asked.

"Both of them."

Chapter 6

FATHER JACOB SAT at a table in a makeshift office inside the downtown hospital, accompanied by two policemen. One of the officers, a plump man with stubby features and receding hairline, sat impatiently in front of him as his fidgeting partner paced the floor holding a cell phone to his ear. The plump cop awkwardly sipped on a cup of coffee trying to not notice Father Jacob's nervous, anxious stare at his partner.

Finally, the pacing policeman lowered the phone and spoke. "They've found only two survivors at the first site."

Father Jacob thought he must have heard him wrong. The officer sounded as if he were reciting a grocery list. He would never understand how people could become so callous in regard to human life.

He asked the officer coldly. "Survivors? Who?"

"Elton and Yates."

"Malcolm Elton?" Father Jacob asked with relief. All had not been lost. "What about the other site?"

"They're still searching." The policeman put his ear back to the phone then spoke again. "They're bringing your men in now."

Father Jacob began making his way to the elevator. He wanted to see Malcolm and the soldier as soon as they got in the building. Maybe they could offer information on where Ramiro was.

"Keep me posted. You have my cell phone number."

⇢▸■◉ ◉■◂⇠

Ramiro lay unconscious on floor of damp, dirty, underground room, bound by chains at his wrists. Standing over him were two men, one wearing an expensive cream-colored suit and the other scrubs. Behind them were three other men built like linebackers.

"Wake him, Doctor," ordered the man in the suit.

The doctor broke a vial of smelling salts under Ramiro's nose, and he awoke.

"Hello, Mr. Vasquez. Do you remember me?" the well-groomed man asked.

Ramiro squinted at him, wincing from a large wound in his chest. His eyes focused on the man. "Yeah. I remember you. Sean Roberts. I was hoping you were dead." He coughed violently, fell over, and moaned as blood oozed from his wound, all of which made the sarcastic smile on Sean's face widen.

Sean motioned to one of the large men, who got a chair and placed it in front of Ramiro. Sean unbuttoned his blazer and sat down. He had chiseled features like a model's but his graying black hair made him look more like a Hollywood playboy. He leaned forward, looking Ramiro directly in the eye. "You know what I want. Where is the he? Where is Ian Khang?"

Ramiro cursed. "You're wasting your time Sean. I don't know where they're keeping him."

Sean chuckled. "Come on, Ramiro. Let's not play that game. I know they're keeping him stateside, and I know that old fool, Father Jacob, is in charge of both the Vatican's organizations here. You can't expect me to believe, he didn't tell the man in charge of his army where the Shaman is."

"Believe what you want. I don't know where he is."

Sean sat back in the chair, shook his head, and played with the cuffs of his shirt. "I'm supposed to torture you now, right? Well, I've gotten bored with the whole torture thing. A man like you would take days to break because you care more about your cause than you do yourself, but . . ."

The door of the cellar flung open and two more henchmen came in dragging two of Ramiro's soldiers. Their faces were swollen with cuts and bruises that had not been there when they were taken.

Sean continued. "But if I put someone's life in your hands . . . things get interesting."

Ramiro regarded the soldiers wearily. He knew he and his men were all going to die whether-or-not he told Sean what he wanted to know or not.

"You son of a bitch!" Ramiro shouted and pulled hard on the chains holding his wrists.

"I'm far worse than that, Ramiro. Yes. I know your real name. I know how long you've worked for Father Jacob. I know your wife died of cancer and that you have a daughter. Lizzy just turned twenty-one, right? You shouldn't be surprised.

You've been watching us. We've watched you too." He laughed smugly. "We use some of the same FBI contacts. I guess you realized that when you attacked the site last night." He sat upright and folded his arms. "Why don't you just tell me where he is and save your men from all that pain?"

Ramiro met his eyes. "Go fuck yourself."

Sean smiled then stood up and buttoned his blazer. He pointed to the smaller of the two soldiers and left the room, as the muscular men in suits began rolling-up their sleeves.

Pain throbbed from Malcolm's forehead as he stood at the window of Lisa's hospital room. The failed raid on the Nesphar's compound was playing over in his head, each scene reminding him of how powerless he felt despite having an automatic weapon in his hands. He kept telling himself the cult members were wearing some sort built proof armor but the truth of what he saw was whispering in argument, blood did spurt and flow when the bullets made contact, kill shots landed flush where major arteries should be. But the men that should have been died did not fall.

Lost in his thoughts, he did not see Lisa, stir and wake in the hospital bed behind him. She squinted hard as if she had been suddenly thrust into light after having lived days in darkness. As her eyes adjusted and the realization of where she was dawned, it was clear she expected to be somewhere else. She moved in the bed, and pain roll from her temples to the front of her forehead. She raised her hand and felt the restricted movement of her arm with the I V inserted in it before noticing Malcolm at the window. She called to him in a weak, dry voice.

Malcolm turned and took her hand into his as he reached her bedside. "Lisa. I'm here, baby." He kissed her cheek. "You're going to be OK, and the doctor said you might have a slight concussion is all."

She placed a hand at his bandage and looked him over, noticing the now purple bruises on his face. He assured her he was OK and surveyed the room.

"Where's Dad? Is he here?"

Malcolm kissed her hand and held it tightly before looking back at her. "Baby—, just rest for now—OK?"

She did not want to believe what his eyes were telling her. "Where is he? I want to see him."

Malcolm took a breath then spoke softly. "They took him."

"No!" Lisa screamed. Her eyes turned red and tears welled.

Malcolm stood and held her as best he could. "We'll find him! I promise! Everything is going to be fine."

"No! They never find them. They never find them! I've seen it!"

Malcolm took his good hand and firmly turned her head toward him. "Have I ever broken a promise to you? Have I?"

"No," she said. Her voice was shaky.

"And I'm not going to start now. I will find him!"

After a few seconds she relaxed in his arms and nodded with a weary expression on her face.

"Mr. Elton," a doctor standing at the door called.

Malcolm cuffed Lisa's cheek then went to Doctor.

The doctor led Malcolm further from the doorway. "I've been told of her situation by Father Jacob. I'm going to give her a mild sedative. I want her as relaxed as possible. There are still tests to run."

"OK. Do what you need to do. How's the guy I came in with? How's Yates doing?"

"I'm sorry, but he didn't make it. He passed earlier this morning. We managed to stabilize him, but he sustained too much trauma to his respiratory system."

The doctor turned and walked away.

Malcolm took a moment to take in what the doctor said. He had struggled to protect the soldier during the battle. He turned to go back into the room.

"Excuse me."

Malcolm looked up to see a policeman had approached him.

"Father Jacob wants to see you downstairs. I've been sent to watch her."

"OK."

As Malcolm turned to go back in the room he saw the policeman unfold a chair he had been carrying and sit down. The chair gave a little from his considerable bulk.

Malcolm kicked the leg of the chair. "This is my woman. I'd prefer if you'd stand. At least act like you give a shit."

The officer shot him an angry look then grunted as he got up.

Malcolm took the chair with him back into the room. "Baby, Father Jacob wants to see me. This officer is going to be outside. If you want to reach me just pick up the phone and dial zero. The operator will connect you. Alright?"

"OK," she replied, hardly noticing him. As he turned to leave, she pushed herself up to ask, "When will you be back?"

He kissed her. "Soon, I promise."

⊷⊨⊜ ⊙⊨⊰⊶

Malcolm passed hallway security and was puzzled by the presence of U.S. soldiers also making their way to Father Jacob's room. As he neared the doorway he noticed the room was filled with soldiers of which only a handful were the Vatican's. He entered the room and began making his way through the crowd. He spotted Father Jacob standing in the front of the room and passed Gallois and Heather standing with the soldiers. He stopped briefly, puzzled by seeing Gallois.

"Malcolm," Father Jacob said, calling him over. "How are you feeling?"

Malcolm lightly rubbed his head bandage. "Fine, just a few scratches, nothing serious."

"And Lisa?"

"They're still running test but they think she will be OK."

"Good, Good. Well, I better get started." He gestured for Malcolm to take a seat before calling out.

"Can I have your attention?" The low murmuring of the soldiers immediately ceased.

"I was told that you all have been briefed on why you're here. You're here to escort us to the airport. We're flying out to a new location in California. When we get there you will join up with more soldiers and a new commanding officer, General Hinshaw. He will be in charge of searching for the Nesphar. We're leaving at nineteen hundred hours. Until then, you will be under the command of Lieutenant Collins here." He gestured to a short, stocky soldier at his side.

Malcolm looked up at Father Jacob, disenchanted. He expected the Vatican to get someone with more experience to handle searching for the Nesphar, but these soldiers were supposed to be under his command until then. He felt like he had been stabbed in the back. Why did Father Jacob overlook Ramiro's wishes to leave him in charge? He could not think of anything that he had done to provoke Father Jacob into doing this.

Father Jacob avoided eye contact as he sat down, and Collins came forward to address the men. All the soldiers in the room came to attention.

"OK, men. I'll save my formal welcoming speech for later. All you need to know for now is that I don't take any shit, but I give it with a vengeance! I want weapons and vehicles checked and ready by twenty hundred hours! Let's make it happen!"

"Sir, yes, sir!" they all answered in unison before leaving the room.

Collins waited for the last man to leave then followed. Heather, Gallois, Father Jacob, and Malcolm were the only ones left sitting.

Malcolm stood. "I guess I've been decommissioned," he said bitterly to Father Jacob.

"Wait a minute Malcolm. I didn't want to assume that you would take over until we had a chance to talk. He looked at Malcolm curiously. "How's your faith, Malcolm?"

"My faith?"

"Yes. I know that you used to attend services regularly. But you haven't been present for quite some time."

"I don't see how my faith has anything to do with this." Father Jacob scoffed.

"It has everything to do with it, son. What do you think you've been doing this whole time? You're a soldier sworn to secrecy for the Vatican."

Malcolm tried to appear confident. "I joined because of my faith. I was told that I would be protecting the Catholic faith."

Father Jacob sat down in his desk chair. "Forget about denominations. It would be more accurate just to say you're protecting religion." He looked at Gallois then back at Malcolm. "There are people with supernatural gifts living among us."

"Supernatural gifts? What do you mean?"

"Gallois," Father Jacob called.

Gallois leaned closer to his mother.

"It's OK. He needs to see," Heather said, standing with her son. Gallois timidly pulled off his gloves and goggles and approached Malcolm with Heather following. He stretched out the palms of his hands.

"Give him your hand, sergeant," Heather said.

Confused, he gave Gallois his hand and laughed. "What is this? Is he going to read my palm?"

Gallois covered Malcolm's hands with his own and closed his eyes in concentration.

"Close your eyes, Malcolm." Father Jacob insisted. Malcolm smirked at him.

"Humor us, son."

A few seconds passed, and suddenly Malcolm had a moment from his past flash through his mind, then again faster and clearer. Suddenly he was a teenager again, sitting in his childhood bedroom. He looked around. A song was playing on his baseball radio next to his bed. This is my old room. He picked up the radio. "My old radio. I broke this." He looked around the room as he placed the radio back on the table.

A pile of baseball cards lay spread out on the bed. "My old collection." He picked up a couple of cards and noticed a calendar on the wall. March 9, 1991, was circled repeatedly in red.

He stopped and dropped the cards. "I remember this day . . . Dad." A shiver ran down his spine.

"Malcolm!" a woman called.

Tears filled his eyes as a teenage version of himself ran from his body and out of the room. Malcolm followed the younger version of himself as it eagerly ran down a hallway and down a staircase. Malcolm sobbed as he neared the end of the steps. His teen self was standing just beyond them in front of his mother and his wheelchair-bound father.

"Malcolm, come here. He's home! Your father's home!" his mother urged.

But teenage Malcolm did not move. He just stared despondently at his father's wheelchair.

"Malcolm?" His mother called again as she stepped forward.

"That's not my father!" teen Malcolm screamed before turning and running back up the stairs.

The vision ended. Gallois had let go of Malcolm's hand. Malcolm was still crying as he had been in the vision. Slowly, it dawned on him that the vision was over.

"Are you all right, Malcolm?" Father Jacob asked. Heather began to speak, but Malcolm grabbed Gallois by the throat and pushed him to the floor.

"What the fuck did you do to me? You freak! You like to fuck with people's minds!" He tightened his grip until Gallois was choking.

"Lieutenant!" Father Jacob yelled.

"Let go of him!" Heather screamed.

When Malcolm noticed that Gallois's eyes were glowing, he released his grip and froze. "What the hell are you?"

Gallois gasped for air.

Father Jacob's face was red. "He's a child, and if I ever see you mistreat him again in any way, I will have you released from duty! Do we understand each other Lieutenant?"

Malcolm took hold of a piece of furniture to help him stand up. "Yes, sir. But you didn't have to do that."

"It was necessary. I wanted you to fully understand what I'm about to tell you." He wiped his brow. "Have you ever heard of the term Stigmata Lieutenant?"

Malcolm nodded. "Yes. It's the mark of those touched by God."

"That's correct. Do you believe in it?"

Malcolm hesitated. "I suppose it's possible."

"No, Lieutenant, it's absolutely possible. Stigmata are rare occurrences of a commonly unaccepted truth that the spiritual world is very real. Without knowing it, we experience angelic and demonic spiritual energy every day, but we only notice it at certain times. You can feel it around you when you're gathered at church or within those seconds of something bad happening. Those wise enough, can see it in the eyes of the redeemed and possessed. There are some people out there like Gallois who are more profoundly affected by that energy. They're able somehow to channel, absorb, and use it."

Malcolm glanced at Gallois. "What does the Nesphar want with them?"

Father Jacob threw up his hand, "I'm getting to that. There're only two types of spiritual energies: angelic and demonic. As you'd probably guess, angelic energy is not harmful. It revives the inner-most thoughts of the person it's used on with the purpose of bringing about truth and understanding. But demonic energy is a tool of the dark forces. Its only objective is to destroy. Now, imagine what would happen if someone could channel and absorb the spiritual energy of not just an evil-hearted man or demon but that of one of the original damned souls. What if a person absorbed the spiritual energy of a fallen angel such as Satan himself?"

Malcolm stammered, "But they're still human right? Wouldn't a bullet kill them just as any other person?"

"No, not always. That's the problem. Demonic forces exist in our world, but they are not of our world. Our rules don't directly apply to them. There are limits on what they can do to us. Being true to their nature, the Damned are always trying to break the rules."

Malcolm paused. "Is that why we couldn't kill those men at the Nesphar compound? Why didn't you warn us? We got slaughtered!"

"Because we thought Xuan was dead. She and Ian have a mental connection that we thought the Nesphar didn't know about. Ian sees what she sees. The last vision Ian had from her was of someone shooting her in the head."

"You still should've made sure we were prepared to fight those things. Instead of guns, I guess we should've had holy water and crucifixes or something!"

Father Jacob slammed his hand on the table. "What makes you so sure I didn't, Lieutenant? I've been doing this for a very long time. Long enough to know there's not much else one can do other than blessing bullets to prepare for demons. With that said, it'd be wise for you to put aside all those Hollywood notions of fighting demons. Human flesh is like armor to demons. It enables them to withstand most religious relics and holy water. They can even walk on holy ground. For any of those things to work you'd have to destroy the human body or exorcise the demon."

Malcolm looked back at Gallois. "Yeah, well, what does he have to do with all this? Why did the Nesphar attack the church?"

"It was Leba. He was after me. I'm the only one who knows where the other Vatican site is, and that's where Ian is being kept. We'll stop at a hotel before we go there, and then I'll tell you exactly where it is." Father Jacob looked to Heather. "Thank you. You two can go and get ready for the flight."

Heather shot a cold look at Malcolm as Father Jacob watched them leave. "Before Ian's last vision of his sister, Ian saw Sean drug her. That same night Gallois's father abducted. Gallois's father was an angel once."

Malcolm's face looked as though he had just learned that the world was really flat. "An angel?"

"Yes, there's a lot more going on here than you know. For now, I'm telling you only what you need to know. Gallois's father's name was Fabian. He chose to live as a human to be with Heather. We don't know why they took him but I didn't want them to get Gallois." Father Jacob took a breath. "I know it's a lot to take in. If you decide to stay I will explain things to you in more detail. If not, then after we leave here you are free to do whatever you want. You can rejoin the regular military. The Vatican will recompense you for your services rendered."

Malcolm thought for a moment. He was confused on so many levels. He could not focus on an answer. Everything he knew about life had been shaken.

"Let me know your decision before we leave." Father Jacob walked by him as he moved toward the door.

"Wait, I'll do it." Malcolm said. "But from now on you tell me everything."

Father Jacob nodded. "Of course, just as I would for Ramiro. You're in charge now." He walked out.

Malcolm sat down. He needed time to think. He had based his decision to stay on his loyalty to Ramiro and his promise to

Lisa. A memory of the last time he had seen Ramiro flashed through his mind. Ramiro believed in him enough to leave him in charge. He did not want to let him down or let the Nesphar get away with taking him. The new information did not change the reasons he had joined the Vatican's army. He still believed in their cause.

Chapter 7

"You sons of bitches! Leave him alone!" Ramiro yelled at Sean's henchmen. They had been torturing the young soldier for well over an hour now. Matt's naked, battered and broken body was sprawled out on the floor. One of the henchmen wielding an aluminum bat lowered it on Matt's shin.

"You ready to talk?" the henchman asked.

"You want to hear something? Give me that bat! I'll make you eat it, you fake-ass tough guy!"

The henchman smiled before slamming the bat down again. Barely alive, Matt's only response was a low moan. The henchmen had beaten every part of his body except his head. Bones from his ribs stuck out through his skin. The guards must have done this many times before. The sight of Matt's body would have sickened any unseasoned spectator.

Ramiro wondered why he had not died already. He was strong. Under the circumstances, it would have been better if he were not.

Ramiro's head throbbed from the stress of witnessing the torture. He looked over at the other soldier across the room.

The soldier sobbed in silence, unable to speak. A dirty white cloth was shoved in his mouth. He had kept his eyes closed most of the time in a desperate attempt to avoid seeing what was in store for him. Ramiro tried to think of a way to turn Sean's attention onto him or at least a way to give them all a quick death. Sean was too smart to fall for anything simple.

He thought to tell him of the old location. He was sure that the Vatican had already moved Ian from his original location, but knowing where that one was might lead them to the real site. Then he had an idea. The Vatican had numerous old safe houses throughout the world. If he could waste enough of Sean's time, maybe he would give up on him and the soldiers. He would try to frustrate Sean into killing them. Sean seemed to be an orderly guy, like Malcolm. Maybe he could make him lose his composure. He would try to unleash the homicidal monster that lurked beneath Sean's elegant surface.

"Stop! All right, I'll tell him what he wants to know."

The guard jerked his head to another guard near the door.

"It's about time," he said. "I was beginning to think that you liked this. What a fucking mess!" He looked over at the gagged soldier. "What do you think? Think he likes it? Sooner or later they all give in." He knelt down and wiped the sweat from Ramiro's head. "You wouldn't believe what he makes us do sometimes. Believe me, this is nothing!"

Ramiro jerked away. "You enjoy being his slave? You have no idea what he's trying to accomplish.

"Whatever it is, I'm sure it will keep him sending money my way, so it's fine with me."

"Even if what he wants will kill your family?"

The guard laughed. "What shit are you talking? What? You gonna tell me that he's after a nuclear weapon or something?"

"That would be a far sight better. You're helping to start the apocalypse, you fool! You're following him right into hell!"

The guard laughed louder. "I haven't even hit you, and you're delirious! Believe me when I say, you don't what to talk like that to Sean. He doesn't have a sense of humor like me."

"Yeah, laugh it up! You'll believe me soon enough."

The door opened, and Sean came in. He walked over and glared at the henchman as he was standing up from Ramiro's side.

"Having a good conversation?"

"No, he was just talking shit," he stuttered.

"So you're finally ready to tell me?" Sean eyed Matt's mangled body as he sat down. "I don't think he could wait much longer. So where is he?"

"I'll tell you if you let us go!"

"Let you go?" Sean asked in surprise.

"Yes. You're going to get what you want, one way or the other. I figure, why not tell you and get something for myself?"

The henchman's eyebrows rose.

"You let us go with some money in our pockets, and I'll tell you."

The guard tried to speak to Sean. Sean made a gesture, and he stopped short. "Well, I'm slightly surprised by your request. You do understand I'm going to need something definite in order to take you seriously, but first, how much money are you asking for?"

Ramiro searched for a believable amount. "Ten million."

"Ten million?"

"Yes, for each of us."

Sean smoothed his hair. "So that's twenty million total." He chuckled. "But I don't think Matt is going to make it. OK, that sounds reasonable. I brought some money just in case you weren't as noble as I thought. Glad I came prepared." He stuck his hand out and then playfully moved it away. "We don't need to shake. You got a deal." He drew a breath. "Go get the man his money."

The guard at the door left the room.

"Anthony, make the man more comfortable." The henchman now had a name. That might come in handy later, Ramiro thought. Anthony unlocked the chains from his wrist.

"Anthony, how long have you known me?"

"For about ten years, sir."

"Would you say that I honor my debts?"

"Yes, sir. Always."

Sean turned. "You see, Ramiro? When it comes to money I'm a man of my word."

Ramiro rubbed his bruised wrists. Anthony walked back over to Sean and handed him a nickel-plated Desert Eagle handgun from his inside coat pocket.

Sean crossed his legs and folded his arms with the gun hanging loosely. "But don't try to back out of this deal."

Ramiro staggered up off of his knees and sat back against the wall. "They've moved him by now."

"Of course," Sean said in an urgent tone.

Ramiro continued, "I can't be sure, but there are only two places they would feel safe keeping him."

Sean's eyes hardened. "This doesn't sound too compelling."

"Just listen, damn it! There are only two places large enough for them to surround him with enough manpower to deter anyone from trying to reach him."

"How much manpower?"

Ramiro stuttered for a brief moment. His voice was dry and forced. "Close to five hundred, maybe a little more."

"You're talking about at each site?"

"Yes."

Sean's brow cursed as his mouth hung open. "Damn! That's a lot of men."

The guard returned with the doctor came in with him, pushing a gurney with an elderly Asian woman lying on it.

"What's this?" Ramiro asked wearily.

"Don't worry about that. Where are the two places?"

"One is here in New York, the other in Virginia." Sean thought for a second, scratching his temple with the gun. "New York? OK. I hadn't considered that." He smiled. "Anthony, old buddy, would you get the man a chair?"

Anthony walked over to a chair.

Bang! Sean shot Anthony in the back of the head. Before his lifeless body could hit the floor, Sean swung around and placed the hot barrel of his gun against Ramiro's temple, burning through to his scalp. "Only an idiot would believe what you're talking about. I would know if the Vatican were assembling that many men. You just want to waste my fucking time!"

Ramiro knew he was right. Sean was a raving lunatic.

Sean held the gun tightly as he spoke. "You think you can wait this out?"

He turned the gun on Matt and shot him in the chest.

"You son of a bitch!" Ramiro yelled and charged at him. Sean had given Ramiro a change for the quick death he wanted. He just hoped to get close enough to break Sean's jaw before being killed. But he did not get a chance to raise his fist before Sean shot him.

Chapter 8

SEAN STOOD OVER Ramiro's body while the doctor checked his pulse. "Is he still alive?"

"Yes. The bullet when straight through. You just missed the artery—the fall must have knocked him out." The doctor pressed down on a gunshot wound on Ramiro's upper left shoulder.

"Wake him."

The doctor slapped Ramiro hard on the face. He woke, startled.

"You still with us?" Sean asked. "I've got someone that I think you were looking for."

The doctor painfully, helped Ramiro to a chair as a henchman wheeled over the woman on the gurney. Ramiro looked at the woman. Her wrinkled, chalk white-skin draped across her face, and she was deadly still. If it were not for the red patches on her forehead, Ramiro would have taken her for a corpse.

"You know who this is? It's Xuan. I didn't kill her as I'm sure you all thought I'd done. I was aware that Father Jacob was using her brother to see through her mind. So the doctor here came up with the perfect solution. Put her into a coma, and then she can be used without any complications." Sean walked behind Ramiro and slid the chair closer to Xuan. "Unfortunately, her body gets tired quickly. When we took Fabian it almost killed her." He looked over at her. "Took years before she was strong enough to be used again." He leaned down close to Ramiro's ear. "I don't think it'll take much for her to get the information I need from you. Leba can be very persuasive. Not to mention I'm sure he's still pissed off at you all."

Ramiro struggled to talk. The pain from the wound pulsated through his chest. "Sean, you of all people should see how fucked up this is. You made her a slave to her abilities after all those years of fearing that yourself. Father Jacob was right. You truly are lost! You think those demons give a damn about you?" Ramiro laughed. "You think you're so smart. Standing there in your expensive suit and manicured nails. You think they consider you, a human, one of them? You'll be the first to die when they finish using you."

Sean tapped the gun hard on Ramiro's head. "Father Jacob's puppet. Save your sermon. I've lived too long to fall for it." He adjusted his suit. "I've done more with my life in ten years than you have in all of yours. I have money, power, and respect. What do you have? You're the lesser man, the commoner, average fucking Joe! Your kind never sees the big picture."

He leaned down to Ramiro's ear. "This shithole God created is one big fucking contradiction for everything written by his so-called prophets. I stopped asking for his help a long time ago, and I've been better off ever since. And as far as rewards go, I'll have my own heaven and I'll build it right on top of the ashes of his."

Sean nodded to the doctor.

The doctor placed a headband with a small round metal device attached to it around Xuan's forehead and stepped away as he took a remote control from his pocket. He pressed a single button on the remote, and electrical currents radiated from the device. Xuan's body began to twitch. As seconds passed, her twitching became more violent.

Ramiro's heart began to race. He had seen Leba manifest himself through Xuan before. Of all the demonic possessions he had witnessed, Leba was the worst demon that he'd seen.

The lights in the room began to flicker. Xuan started breathing heavily.

He tried to push the chair away from her. He knew that her possession was worsened by her inability to fight it off. In a jolt her eyes opened, her pupils so dilated they appeared black.

"Help! Help me!" It was Xuan. Only her mouth moved.

"Xuan?" Ramiro called.

Suddenly Xuan screamed as if she were on fire. Her body thrashed about on the table. Her eyes started bleeding. She pressed hard on them with her hands. Ramiro reached for her, wanting to help, but he knew whatever they had done to her was beyond his control. To his horror, he could only watch her suffer.

Suddenly her body became ridged and a ghostly howl resonated from within her. Her joints tightened as an entity moved underneath her skin and spread throughout her body. She began to convulse.

Her bones broke as her arms and legs stretched out, ripping the hospital gown she was wearing. Xuan screamed louder. Her skin grew even paler and her voice took on a deep, raspy tone.

Ramiro smelled the sickening odor of sulfur and decaying flesh and saw the blood around her eyes turn black.

She slowly rose and sat up on the edge of the stretcher. Her feet were flush on the floor. She was now nearly seven feet tall. Her head slowly turned in Ramiro's direction with a deep snarl that made him rear back in his seat.

Abruptly the creature rushed him. Ramiro threw his body from the chair and scurried backwards, but the intense pain from his wound prevented him from moving far. Leba grabbed him by the shirt, and lifted him off his feet, and brought him to face level. Ramiro turned his face away.

"Ramiro!" Leba hissed. "Waited long, have I, to experience your flesh!" He smelled Ramiro, and then licked his face. "You thought your priest could drive me out! I told you this body belongs to me!"

Ramiro looked at him boldly, defying the terror he felt. "Even if you find him, the angels will stop you. You will never walk this earth, you parasite!"

Leba shoved a finger into the wound on Ramiro's chest. "The angels' time has already ended! Soon they will be bled and abolished!" He twisted his finger deeper into the wound.

Ramiro muffled his scream not wanting to give the beast the satisfaction.

"Through your pain your mind will weaken. Show me where they keep him!"

Ramiro felt Leba searching through his mind. He tried to think of everything except where Ian was.

Leba pressed harder into the wound, twisting his finger. Suddenly a desert flashed through his mind. The vision got clearer. Ramiro screamed as he tried to stop his thoughts. A hotel flashed in his mind, followed by a large building in the desert.

Leba pulled his finger out and laughed as he dropped Ramiro to the ground. "Weak!" Leba hissed as he turned and walked toward Sean and the doctor.

Ramiro cursed himself as he regained his senses watching Leba's as he walked away. In a last futile effort he picked up the chair and smashed it over Leba's head. Leba turned and knocked it away and then grabbed Ramiro's arm and broke it. Ramiro yelled in pain and fell face first to the floor.

Leba snarled as he raised his foot over Ramiro's head.

"Don't!" Sean commanded.

Leba growled and raised his foot higher.

"I said don't! I still need him!"

Leba hissed again and turned to him angrily. "Your delay angers him, fleshling! Again, you have misused the girl! She needs to be strong when you have him!"

Sean stepped forward. "It would have taken longer to get the location out of him. He'd die before he'd told us."

Leba approached him and the trembling doctor distanced himself from Sean.

"You are unworthy of his service!"

Sean frowned arrogantly. "Really? Well, you can do this on your own then."

Leba grabbed him by the throat and lifted him from the floor.

"Go ahead! Do it! And you can stay in hell!" Sean chocked out.

The doctor moved farther away.

Leba tightened his grip and then released him.

Sean fell to his knees and regained his breath before standing and fixing his suit. He muffled a curse. "Well? Where is he?"

Leba smiled before answering, "In the Mojave Desert, there is a structure at the foot of the widest canyon. They call it Oasis. The old man is there."

Sean turned his back on Leba and walked toward the doctor. "Let her rest now. We'll have him soon."

Leba barked angrily as he lay back on the gurney. "You won't be able to kill the half-breed! Bring me some willing souls."

"Do it!" Sean said to the doctor as he walked away.

Chapter 9

A FASTEN SEATBELT sign flashed as the 747 passenger plane shook and dipped in turbulence. A bell chimed and the pilot's voice sounded through the loud speakers, announcing they were preparing to land and asking for the passengers to remain seated until the plane came to a complete stop. Then he ended the announcement with a joke about the airline food before thanking them for choosing the airline.

But the last thing Malcom felt like doing was laughing as he scowled at Gallois sitting in the row of seats across from him and Lisa. He had not been able to think about anything but his father since he had boarded along with the shame of turning his back on the man when he returned from the war. It had happened years ago, long before he had learned to deal with his father's condition and months before his father's injuries caused his death. But the shame he felt that day had never left. Now this freak had caused him to re-experience it. He had never liked that freak and now he was sure he never would.

Gallois's head turned in his direction, and he looked away, pretending to be gazing out the window also. After a few seconds, he turned back and found Gallois's black, tinted goggles on him. He looked back to the window. His heart was beating fast. He wondered if Gallois were doing something to him. In his peripheral vision, he could see the freak was still looking at him. Could he hear his thoughts?

After a few seconds, Gallois's head slowly turned back to the window. But Malcolm dared not look in his direction again. He kept staring out the tiny window, trapped in the memory that must have devastated his father.

Lisa leaned into him. "It's so weird seeing him outside that room," she said, looking at Gallois.

"Yeah. He's been staring out that window the whole flight. I didn't realize clouds were so interesting."

"I've never really thought about it."

"Thought about what?"

"He's been in that room his whole life." Her head lowered. "I never really thought about what it must have been like for him to live like that." She put her hand over his. "Dad would've loved to see this."

He squeezed her hand and was about to agree with her before she cut him off.

"I want to join the Vatican's army."

Malcolm sighed. He had dreaded this moment but had known it was coming. Her father let her train with the army, but he had repeatedly said, he did not want her to join. He wanted her to attend college and have a safe and stable life.

"You know your father didn't want that."

"They took him. Just like they took Gallois's father. I'm not going to let them get away with that."

"Your father wanted a different life for you. You should do what would've made him happy. I will make sure the Nesphar pay for what they have done."

Lisa turned away and returned her gaze to Gallois. "How can I? Everything's different now. I can't pretend that it's not."

He leaned into her. "No. I know that, baby. I'm just saying you should try. For your father, just try."

She looked at him with a well of sadness in her eyes then turned away again. He did not know what that meant. He did not say more because he did not want to press the issue and get into an argument. Besides, he was in charge of the army now, and she could not join without his approval. If she filled out the paper, he would drag the process out long enough for her to reconsider. She was hurting and just needed time to think. He was sure she would honor her father's wishes.

The plane landed not long after, and they loaded their luggage into jeeps and made their way to a hotel that was to be their last stop before going to the new location.

Las Vegas, Nevada.

Gallois sighed as he laid his head against the glass window of his hotel room. He looked down at the grass below. He was on the tenth floor, but it seemed higher. He looked to his right, near the sidewalk closest to the street, and wondered at the people going about their business as he had done thousands of times at the church. The weight of his head caused the unlocked window to swing open. He pushed the window open as far as it would allow and stuck his head out to her an orchestra of sounds that was new to him: the hum of automobile engines, horns, and indistinct voices.

Teenagers appeared from the corner of the building wearing long baggy pants and colorful shoes and riding skateboards. He watched them at length as they laughed while attempting tricks on the handicapped ramp and handrail of the hotel's side entrance. He wondered what they were talking about between tricks and how they'd come to be friends. He imagined being friends with them. He wondered what they'd say if he approached them. Would they like him and want to be friends?

He pulled off his goggles and clasped a hand over his eyes to see if they were aglow. Thankfully, they weren't, and he continued looking at the skateboarders, waiting for an opportunity to yell, "Awesome trick, dude!" which he'd read a teenager say in one of his favorite books. He practiced saying the words several times until it sounded just right. He was up pretty high up, so he was going to have yell it really loudly for them to hear him. But before the opportunity arrived, the teens skated away down the sidewalk and vanished from view.

Gallois dragged his head back inside the window, pulled the window shut and, saw his reflection in the glass. Why do I always look so sad? No one would want to be friends with someone who looks so depressed.

He smiled, but it did not look natural no matter how many times he tried. Finally he gave up and frowned at his reflection. I look like something's wrong with me, like I'm some sort of weirdo. His eyes illuminated as if they were mocking him. He slung his goggles at the wall on the other side of the room and then punched the window frame hard, hoping to hurt himself.

But the frame was the only thing damaged. Three knuckle imprints were left in the wood. He could not even do that right. His freak of a body would not allow it. He dropped his head back against the window and noticed couples walking hand-in-hand on the sidewalk as he had seen Lisa and Malcolm do. He tried imagining himself walking in the same way with someone he loved, something he had envisioned hundreds of times while reading novels. But after seeing this real-life version he could not imagine anything. He watched the couples until he could not see them anymore, and then turned his gaze back to the street.

What is it like to live as you do? You're all the same, nothing strange or unusual. Why did I have to be born different? I'd give anything to be like you, to be normal. Then you'd accept me. You wouldn't be afraid to talk to me or to be my friend. You wouldn't watch me with that stare as if you're adding up all the ways I don't fit in.

I wonder what my life would been like if I weren't born this way. I'd probably be a totally different person. All I've known in my life is living with being different. I can't even imagine a real life.

It doesn't matter anyway. I'll always be this way. What kind of life will I have? How am I going to ever be happy? I'll never have a wife or a family. One day my mom will die then. . . Mom. I want her to be happy before that time comes. She should've left me a long time ago. I'm keeping her from happiness. She could have a normal life, but she's stuck with me. She won't leave because of me!

She's been through enough pain in her life. She deserves better. But how could I ever convince her to leave? She wouldn't leave even if I begged her. I'd have to die first. It'd be better for her if I were dead!

He imagined his mother grieving over his casket. But then she'd be in pain like when my father was taken. Still, would it be so bad? All these years she's been living in fear. Fear of the Nesphar's coming and taking me. She could finally get past it. Besides, how do they even know that the Nesphar wants me? The soldier that night said the demons were looking for Father Jacob, not me. And why do they get to make all the decisions for me anyway?

It's my life. I'm sixteen, old enough to make my own decisions. I don't want to keep hiding. I can take care of myself. I stopped them easily that night at home. I can be what I am without all this hiding. If they want me to stay away from people outside the church, I will but I don't see why I can't have at least some of the things I want.

As questions he had never asked himself flooded his mind, new possibilities seemed to present themselves. He wondered why he had never thought this way before. He was getting older, becoming a man, a full grown adult. His mother and Father Jacob could not keep telling him what to do. Letting himself imagine such freedom, he slid opened the window and straddled himself on the window sill, letting an arm and leg dangle outside it.

His mother would tell him to come back inside if she were here. But she was not and this was his room, his own room, and he could do what he wanted in it. He raised and lowered his arm, feeling the wind flow over his skin. He leaned his whole upper body out the window, only his leg kept him from falling out. For anyone else this would be dangerous. But it was not for him. His freak body was good for something.

He gazed up beyond the skyscrapers at the moon and stars, imagining the view from up there. He wondered what it would feel like to fly up there. He closed his eyes and raised both arms, allowing himself to feel the freedom of open space, and leaned further until he felt as if he would slip and fall out.

"Gallois?" Lisa called standing in the doorway. "What are you doing?" Judging by the look on her face, he knew what she must be thinking. If she had entered a few minutes earlier she would be right. He smiled the best he could and spoke in a playful tone.

"Nothing. Goofing off." He pulled his limbs back inside the window.

She gave him a careful stare and seemed to disregard her previous thoughts. She entered the room and brushed hair behind her ear as she always did when she was nervous about something. "Can I talk to you?" she asked, closing the door behind her.

He nodded, and she sat down beside him. Her eyes were red.

"Are you okay?" he asked.

She stared at his uncovered eyes and smiled. "This is going to take some getting used to." She placed a hand on his face. "You have beautiful eyes."

"Thanks," he replied with a faint smile.

Lisa pushed more hair behind her other ear. "I'm sorry. I must look a real mess right now."

"It's okay. I know how you feel."

"Yeah, you do, don't you?" She sniffed. "It doesn't seem real. One minute he's here then the next gone, just like that."

"Malcolm will find him," Gallois said, trying to sound optimistic.

She lowered her head. "He keeps telling me that. I wish I could believe him. But you know they never find them. They try, but they never do." She placed a hand on his knee. "I'd imagined many times how it must feel for you and your mother. It's a whole lot worse than I thought." She started to cry.

He hugged her, not knowing what else to do.

"Why did this happen to them? They're good men. They didn't deserve this. The Nesphar are going to pay for what they've done. Dad was right! The Vatican always waits until something like this happens before they do anything. Well, fuck them!"

As he watched to her rant, a scar appeared to him on her face. His eyes illuminated. Her hate was becoming visual to him.

"Don't let them change you," he said. But she didn't hear. She did notice his glowing eyes and flinched. Gallois stood up and grabbed his goggles from the floor.

"No, don't," Lisa protested, grabbing his arm and taking the goggles from him.

He could not look at her. He waited for her scream and run away, but she stepped closer instead.

"How?" she asked.

His mouth opened but he said nothing.

She gently took his face in her hands. "So that's the real reason you wear them."

She fell silent for several seconds, and Gallois could see her putting all the horrible pieces together.

"I thought I was going crazy," she said. "I didn't tell Father Jacob about those men or the things I saw them do. But he already knew, didn't he? And you do too? Those things, you know what they were, don't you?

He hesitated, not wanting to scare her but sensing she wanted confirmation of what she already knew. He could not bring himself to tell her. The thought of her father's being at the mercy of demons would be too much. All these years he had to live with that. He wanted to spare her that truth as long as he could. But he could not lie to her now. Not about her father. She deserved to know.

His voice was soft. "They were demons."

She dropped to her knees, crying with her arms clutched around her chest as if the pain she felt were trying to bust out of her. He got to his knees and hugged her, and minutes passed before she suddenly stopped crying.

"All these years," she said. "Why didn't you tell me you weren't sick? I thought we were friends. I thought we trusted each other."

"I do trust you." he said. "They said telling you would put you in danger." That was almost the truth. He remembered the day she had asked why he could not leave the chamber. He was going to tell her truth, but he decided he would rather she had pity him than to think of him as strange. To her, he was a normal boy, not some weird thing in a glass chamber to be stared at.

"That's a lie," she snapped. "They said not to tell me. So what? We've kept secrets. You could have told me."

Gallois fidgeted.

"I didn't want you to be afraid of me," he said, feeling a weight leave his shoulders. His words seemed to sway her anger, but only a little.

"Why would you think that? I could never be afraid of you. You're my best friend."

The comment made Gallois happy. There was a time when he felt he was her best friend, but, as they grew older, her world expanded and he felt he had been replaced.

"You said 'they'," she said. "I know your mom. Who else my, dad?"

"No, Father Jacob."

"So Dad didn't know either?"

"No."

Lisa's eyes went fiery. "How could he keep that from us? Dad should've been told."

"He was trying to protect us."

"Protect us?" She raised the goggles in her hand and squeezed them so hard he thought they would break. "Lies don't protect; they destroy. If he wanted to protect us he should have stopped the Nesphar before this happened or moved us out of that deathtrap he called a church." She threw his goggles on the bed and left, slamming the door behind her.

->|==() ()==|<-

Malcolm hung up his cell phone and cursed. Father Jacob had told him that Lisa had just left his room after asking him to join the Knights. She tried to go over his head, and he should have known that she would.

He squeezed the railing in front of him at the thought of her being killed.

If she did join, how could he focus on the job with her around? She would compromise his every decision. Fortunately, Father Jacob followed the rules and told her to ask him. All he could do was stall her, and that would not work for long. Her mind was made up and she would not stop asking until she had her way. The hopelessness of predicament made his head ache.

He pulled his pack of cigarettes from his pocket and smoked while watching Heather and some teenagers from the monastery loading luggage into one of the transport vehicles.

"Sir," an approaching soldier called.

"Yes, soldier."

"I'm Seth Howard, sir."

Malcom pulled on the cigarette and then exhaled smoke. "Yes, I know who you are. I got your papers. You want to be released from duty, correct?"

"That's correct, sir."

Malcom flicked ash from the end of the cigarette. "You were involved with the hostile situation back at the church?"

"Yes, sir."

"Your file shows that was your first confrontation. Must have been too much for you?" He didn't wait for Seth to answer. "It's good you decided to resign. But I'm confused about what you thought when signed up to do a soldier's work. What did you expect?"

"Sir, may I speak freely? Sir."

"Go ahead, soldier."

Seth widened his stance and clasped his hands behind his back. "Sir, back at the monastery I saw something . . . unnatural."

"Yeah, that's right, soldier. You saw battle."

"No, sir. You don't understand. Those men, they—"

"I'm aware of what you saw. I read the report." Malcolm faced the soldier squarely. "Regardless of what you saw, you're protecting civilians. Isn't that part of the reason you signed on?"

"Yes, sir."

"If your convictions haven't changed, then it must be your nerve. You saw a battle, and you got scared, plain and simple. But hell, soldier, you're doing me a favor by resigning. I don't need any weak-willed soldiers in my unit. Signing your release papers will be my number one priority once we get to where we are going."

The soldier said nothing.

"Do you think you can keep your fear in check long enough to finish your current duty?"

Seth nodded slowly.

"Good. Go to it, soldier."

With that, Malcolm walked away. Honestly, he did not blame the soldier for wanting to leave. The thought had even crossed his mind. When he enlisted into the Vatican's army they said he would see some unusual things. Until the siege on the Nasphar's compound he thought they were talking about exorcisms.

Another soldier came running up to him out of breath. "Sir, I've just got word four large unmarked vans are headed this way."

"We were told there wouldn't be any major transports passing by this area. Make sure all the vehicles are fueled. Leave everything that isn't already packed. We're leaving now."

The soldier saluted and ran off. Malcolm grabbed another soldier by the shoulder. "Get everyone upstairs down here now!"

As the soldier left, Malcolm saw Heather standing with the children holding a box obviously, confused by the sudden movements of the soldiers around her. He turned away before she noticed him. Sadness filled his heart. They had broken him. They didn't need him now. Ramiro was dead.

Four unmarked vans swerved through traffic as they sped up to the entrance of the hotel. Pedestrians and valet attendants yelled as they jumped out of the way. The tires of the vans screeched as they all came to a stop. Men in the front seats of each vehicle pushed a button on the dashboard, and the back doors of the vans opened. Possessed men wearing prison uniforms poured out. They howled and screamed as they ran on all fours toward the entrance, knocking people out of their path.

Lisa pushed open the door before Gallois could hide in the room. Her eyes were wide and an automatic weapon was clutched in her hand,

"Gallois, they're here! We've got to get down stairs to the jeeps."

He looked at her noting her fear.

"You go. I'm staying."

"What? They'll kill you."

He looked at her face. This was the last time he'd ever see it. "I can't go back to that room. I can't hide anymore. Tell Mom I'm sorry."

Tears formed in her eyes and fell when she shook her head. "No! You're coming with me." She said walked over and grabbed his arm.

He pulled away hard enough to let her know he meant it and for her to understand she wasn't strong enough to force him to go.

"I'm staying." He looked at the door then back at her. "You should go."

The torment of the decision to leave him or stay was on her reddened face, "Gallois, please," she begged, and the sight of it made him cry too.

He kissed her cheek. "Thanks for being my friend. I love you."

Lisa backed away with a lost look in her eyes and Gallois thought she was going to leave but she did not. She dropped her suitcase on the bed.

"I love you too," she said. "And I'd never let you die alone."

Gallois stood up. "No. Lisa, go."

Lisa looked over her shoulder as she aimed her weapon at the door. "Let's not spend our last seconds arguing." Gallois's eyes were wide as the thought of her being ripped apart by the demons dawned on him. He wouldn't let that happen. He had to get her out of there.

"OK. Let's go."

Lisa grabbed him by the wrist, and they ran out of the room.

Father Jacob and two soldiers waited eagerly for the elevator to reach the basement. But the elevator stopped.

"What's wrong?" he asked one of the Knights pressing buttons.

"I don't know," The Knight answered.

Something heavy landed on the roof of the elevator fallowed by growling noises above and below.

"Something's out there!" The Knights cocked their guns and listened as the noise traveled around the elevator car.

"Get down!" a Knight commanded, pushing Father Jacob to his knees.

He crouched between both of the Knights. With a loud crash, the elevator ceiling hatch was ripped away and a ghoulish face with sharp fangs looked down at them. The Knights began firing rounds at the hatch.

"Dear Lord!" Father Jacob screamed, crouching lower and covering his ears as bullet shells bounced off his head.

"It's stopped on the fourteenth floor," Malcolm said, watching the level display as he stood with his men in the basement facing the elevator door. "How many are there?" he asked a Knight.

"Three vans that size can carry forty, maybe forty-five men."

Malcolm considered his options. He did not want to risk his men's lives. The chances of saving anyone upstairs were slim. He was not trying to protect vital information anymore. If the Nesphar knew they were here, they probably already knew the location of the second safe house. His only job now was to save as many lives as he could.

"Wait!" a soldier yelled. "Listen, you hear that?"

They all listened. To the array of muffled growls.

"It's coming from the elevator shaft!"

Malcolm approached the elevator door and pressed his ear to it. He quickly jumped back, aiming his gun at the door. "Everybody, get ready!"

Loud thuds sounded behind the door, followed by terrible howls and bellows. The already nervous soldiers' excitement intensified as they aimed their weapons impatiently.

The possessed people began forcing the shaft door open. When the first ghoulish face became visible, the soldiers did not wait for the command to shoot.

⇥⊨◉ ◉⊨⇤

Lisa pressed on the elevator button, but she could not hear any cars moving. "Shit! Come on, we'll take the stairs," she said.

They ran down the hall, passing a couple trying to open their room door. Gallois pulled on Lisa's arm, stopping her midway to the stairwell. "We're too late. They're coming."

The doors of the stairwell flung, open and the possessed men began filling the hall. Gallois and Lisa turned around and ran toward the couple standing at their room door. The woman screamed, seeing the possessed men in pursuit and yelled for the guy to open the door. Gallois had just made it past them when they saw demons forcing their way through the elevator door on the other side of the hall. Their only option now was to get inside the couple's room.

"Open it! Hurry up!" Lisa shouted.

The man fumbled some more before finally getting the door open and they stormed in the room, slamming the door behind them.

"Help me!" Lisa said to the guy, struggling with a dresser.

Gallois and the girl stood off at a distance. The possessed men began banging on the door. The door frame shook and cracked from the weight of the creature's bodies. It was not going to hold them back for long. Lisa and young man managed to overturn the dresser, but moving it on the carpeted floor was difficult.

Gallois forced them out of the way and pushed the dresser against the door just before the hinges could break. One of the possessed men was caught in the broken door. It squeezed its way through and ran toward Lisa and the tall young man. He grabbed a lamp from a table, but before he had a chance to swing it, the possessed man knocked him aside and continued in Lisa's direction.

"Get back!" Lisa screamed, pushing the girl out of the way. She fired her weapon. The possessed man took most of the bullets to its chest but kept coming. Lisa's gun clip went empty and her eyes widened. As the possessed man charged again, she slipped a hand into her pocket and pulled out a grenade.

Gallois appeared behind the creature. He grabbed it in an arm lock and tossed it to a wall.

"Get the door!" Gallois shouted.

Lisa ran back to the door with the girl following her. The skinny guy scrambled to his feet and helped them. They sat on the floor with their backs to dresser, watching as the possessed man got up and lunged for Gallois.

Gallois parried then punched the creature in the throat and floored it with a push kick.

"We can't hold them!" Lisa yelled as she and the others were being inched forward by the demons' efforts.

Gallois grabbed a pen from the floor as the creature got to its feet to attack again. When it lunged at him once more, he stabbed it in the eye with the pen. After a shriek and a spray of blood and gray ooze, the creature fell lifeless to the floor, sending Gallois into a brief stupor from which Lisa's scream woke him.

He stepped over the creature's body and grabbed the couple by the arms. He pulled them to their feet and pointed to the bathroom. "You'll be safe in here," he said. "They're after me, not you."

The guy hesitated, fixated on Gallois's illuminated eyes.

"Go on!"

The couple did as they were told and Gallois went back to Lisa.

"Let them in," he said.

"You can't fight them all."

"I know. Come on."

She got to her feet and stood with him. They walked backwards as the dresser inched forward and the first demons began pushing their way through. Lisa reached for Gallois's hand and held it firmly. Raised in her other hand was the grenade.

"No," Gallois said, pushing her hand down. He grabbed a chair and threw it through the window behind them. The hinges finally broke, and the door fell onto the dresser. Possessed men began pouring into the room. Gallois pulled Lisa close to him and backed closer to the window's edge. When the possessed charged, Gallois took Lisa by the waist and pulled the two of them out the window.

Lisa screamed hysterically as they fell, watching as the window rapidly fell from sight behind several falling creatures. Her body flailed about as Gallois struggled to hold onto her. He managed to turn their bodies around toward the rapidly approaching ground, which made Lisa scream louder.

He got her into a cradled position, and she clung to him like a constrictor. Light brown wings sprouted from the open slits in Gallois's shirt, stopping their fall. They glided away from the hotel, leaving the screaming creatures in their freefall. Lisa looked down at the ground, first with caution then with disbelief. Emotionally used up, she nestled her head back on Gallois's chest and loosened her grip as he thrust with his wings to take them higher.

Chapter 10

MALCOLM FELT A weight stirring in his stomach as he surveyed his men in the large van. They had barely escaped the hotel. He had to leave without Lisa and Gallois, and the choice was burning a hole through him. He wanted to scream and slam his fist into the floor board. But he was in charge of the Knights now. He had to be the strong leader like Ramiro and get everyone to safety.

"Any word from the site?" he asked a soldier holding a radio.

"No, sir. Nothing. What if we don't reach them in time?"

Malcolm was sure the site was already destroyed and Ian had been kidnapped. But they had to make sure. He would contact the Vatican once they arrived.

"We'll cross that bridge when we get to it," Malcolm answered over the screams of a Knight being stitched and bandaged.

The radioman nodded. Malcolm found another place to sit, away from the eyes of his men. He realized he was still holding his gun. He unloaded it and placed it to the side then lowered his head.

I'm sorry, baby. You were right. I couldn't protect you."

Tears began to well in his eyes. He put a hand on his forehead and nonchalantly wiped his tears.

He spotted Heather sitting on the floor at the other end of the van. Her face was wet with tears as she stared at the floor. His heart sank even lower. He had failed her too. Her only child was gone, and he could not stop it from happening. He lowered his head again and searched for his pack of cigarettes. He felt his cell phone in one of his pockets, pulled it out, and stared at the dial. She wouldn't answer but he had to try. He pressed her number on speed dial.

Gallois flew aimlessly in the night with Lisa cradled in his arms. Air wisped past his ears as his wings rhythmically rose and fell, creating a sound that he briefly mistook for his own heartbeat. He looked around. They were alone in the moonlight; below them were city lights of orange yellow and white. He did not know where they were or how safe they were. The only thing he was sure of was that he had to fly high enough to avoid being seen.

"Keep them tucked," his mother would say about his wings. They burned and ached when he kept them tucked for too long. He could not wait until it was late at night. He would turn off the lights, unfold his wings and fly as much he could in the limited space of his chamber. But now there was nothing restricting him. No wooden beams above and no glass walls to bump into. He felt something loosen in his chest as he gazed up at moon and the stars peeking at him through the thick clouds.

He'd dreamed of seeing them this way. He imagined what the clouds would feel like as he passed through them, wondered how close he could get to the moon. He kept his eyes on the moon as he thrust his wings and began climbing higher and higher.

Lisa's cell phone disturbed the silence with its jaunty ring tone. She moved in his arms then pointed for him to land. They alit on the roof a small building, and he carefully sat her down. She stepped back as she fumbled her cell phone from her pocket while looking at him as if he were a stranger. She pressed a button on her phone and put it to her ear,

"Malcolm?" she sounded relieved. "You're all right? Yes, we are OK. Gallois is right here. Did everyone get out?"

Gallois moved in closer upon hearing his mother's name. He feared what she'd say to him next.

"She's OK. He got her out in time—she's with him." she said.

Relieved, Gallois watched her as she turned her head back into the phone. After a brief exchange Malcolm told Lisa where he was taking his mother and the others. From using his clairvoyance on Malcom at the hospital, he remembered seeing a building in the desert. It had been only flash of a vision, but as usual it was enough. He know exactly how to get to there. He tapped Lisa on the shoulder,

"I know where they're going," he said.

Lisa seemed puzzled, but after he assured her with a nod, she put the phone back to her ear. "We'll be there." She hung up and returned it to her pocket before allowing Gallois to carry her into the sky again.

⊷═▶ ◀═⊶

The vans kicked up sand as they made their way to the site.

"Sir!" a soldier called.

Malcolm rose from beside Heather, who was resting on a mat.

"We're here," said the driver.

Malcolm flicked on the vehicle's fog lights and looked out the window. The beam of light on the horizon slowly revealed what seemed to be a ten-level concrete structure. Its walls were slightly darker than the sand. The place looked more like a giant blast bunker than any military building he had ever seen.

The vehicle slowed, and his eyes widened when the structure's grounds came into full view. At least sixty corpses lay scattered in the sand. There was no movement other than fire and smoke rising from the dead and destroyed vehicles. A large blast door were ajar with blood trails toward a destroyed section of the gate. That was how the Nesphar had escaped with Ian, he realized. And the broken window near the top of the structure revealed how they had entered the site. The building was made to defend against men, not unnatural creatures that climbed walls.

"Stop at the gate entrance," he said. "We'll check the grounds." He knew he wouldn't find anyone alive or any remaining creatures. The Nesphar had whom they had come for. They would not return.

He went to the rear of the van, where most of the Knights had gathered. "I need every man not badly injured," he said. "Call the other vans and tell them to bring only high-caliber weapons."

The vans stopped outside the gate, and Malcolm and the Knights piled out of the vehicles. They reached the dead and began stepping over them with fog lights shining as if in some sadistic theater. Vomit stung at the back of his throat. The soldiers had not died by gunfire. They had been savagely bitten through and torn apart.

This was no way for anyone to die. His only comfort was in the number, though they were few, of possessed that lay dead with them. They wore the same orange prison uniforms as the possessed had back at the hotel.

A soldier looking up into the sky cried out, and everyone went on alert.

Malcolm ran over to the soldier and followed his gaze. He saw the reason for the soldier's alarm. There was a dark shape growing in size.

"Hostile aircraft! Take cover!" he shouted, posting up and taking aim from behind the cover of a van.

The Knights scrambled, took up positions, and aimed their weapons at the figure.

"Wait, don't shoot! It's them!" Heather yelled, running from one of the vans.

Confused, Malcolm raised his an arm and opened his palm, and the soldiers reluctantly lowered their weapons. He gasped when he saw Gallois glide down into the light with Lisa cradled in his arms. And he nearly dropped his weapon with the realization of what was arching out from Gallois' back. He watched them land and Gallois lower Lisa onto the sand. Her eyes searched the slowly approaching Knights. He wanted to go to her, but he could not move. His eyes were stuck on Gallois. It wasn't until she spotted him that he was able to move. He walked over to her as she ran. When they reached each other, he hugged her tightly.

"Are you alright?" he asked.

"I'm fine."

Over her shoulder, he saw Gallois and his mother hugging. The Knights had formed a circle around them, and Gallois' head was buried into his mother's shoulder. Malcom thought he was crying, but when his mother coaxed his head away he saw a fear that mirrored his own in the boy's glowing eyes.

Chapter 11

SEAN'S HENCHMEN PUSHED a wheelchair- bound, elderly Asian man into the large, crudely built space. The old man was gaged. His forearms and hands dangled in his lap. His head lay to one side and bobbed with every bump as his weak, dark eyes surveyed his surroundings. The floor and walls were made of earth. Thick tree roots lined the walls and climbed up 500 feet above where two concreate support beams crossed below a ceiling glass that was too dirty to allow sunlight to shine through. In the center of the room was a large pit, and next to that was a gurney with bed restraints. A pentacle had been drawn beneath it in a red liquid that smelled like wet pennies. The old man screamed into his gag but other than the bobbing of his head, he did not move.

The man wheeled the old man to the gurney, picked him, and strapped him down. Sean and the doctor entered the room and walked past the gurney without looking in their direction.

"Is she ready?" Sean asked the doctor.

"Yes. But I think we should've given her another day or two of rest."

Sean frowned. "Do you want to explain to them why we didn't proceed after capturing Xuan's brother?"

The doctor just stared at him.

Sean chuckled. "I didn't think so. We'll do it tonight."

"What about the angels? When the demons cross over are you sure the angels won't know?"

Sean drew a breath. "Doctor, you're suddenly full of worries, and it's very tiresome." He pointed at the ground. "This pit is where Satan fell when God cast him out. It's cursed ground already. The angels won't sense any disturbance as long as we stay inside this room. After we perform the resurrection, it won't matter if they know or not. Are the weapons prepared?"

"Yes. I did it myself."

"Good."

"Um, have you considered—"

Sean exhaled. "What's to stop them from killing us once they've crossed over? Of course I have. They can't survive in our world without human bodies. There will be six of them and six of us. They'll have to use our bodies, and once they inhabit a body they're bound to it. So our well-being will be theirs." He cast a curious eye on the old man. "He's not afraid."

"I drugged him. He doesn't realize what's about to happen."

"What about when he sees his sister?"

"I'm not sure. That's why he's restrained."

The Oasis Compound.

Malcolm sat with the phone to his ear in what was supposed to be Father Jacob's office. The Vatican representative on the other end spoke in a thick Italian accent and was not bothering to be polite. Malcolm had been biting his tongue for nearly eight minutes now. He looked at Lisa standing by the broken, blood-stained window. The sun was rising. It was too early to be yelled at, especially by someone he did not know. He ground his molars as he continued listening to the bureaucrat bark out orders and profess his disapproval of the "current situation" without much regard for the death of Father Jacob or the Knights.

Finally, the man paused for a breath. He quickly told the representative that they needed time to prepare the bodies of the dead for transport. And they needed him to send enough men to repair the facility and supplies to reinforce vulnerable areas. When he was done, he gave the representative a hasty goodbye and hung up. He rubbed his forehead and turned to Lisa.

"They're sending in Marines," he said.

"Marines?" Bags puffed out from beneath her eyes, and her hair was still wet. She looked as if she had gotten about as much sleep as he had.

"Yeah. Apparently they have connections with the U.S. Military. He didn't give me any particulars, but I think they're Knights like us but some elite branch like black ops. They're going to help look for the Ian. I don't know exactly what it is this Ian can do. But whatever it is, it's got them scared." He walked over to the window and stood next to her. The first rays of sun were stretching on the terrain and there wasn't a cloud in the sky. He looked down at Knights using a firehose to wash the ground and walls clean of blood. "They've been working throughout the night. I'll let them get some rest before the others get here. There's no telling what they'll have us doing."

"What about Gallois and his mother?"

"They'll be fine here. We all will. They're bringing in tanks." He watched Lisa as the look on her face suggested she was thinking the tanks should have already been there. She looked down at the cup of coffee in her hand, sipped, and then looked out the window again. He walked over to the coffee maker to pour himself a cup.

"You should've seen him," she said.

"You mean Gallois?"

"Yeah. He fought those things with his bare hands. If it weren't for him, I'd be dead."

"Don't do that. You're alive. That's all that matters." He finished pouring his coffee and turned around to see Lisa was wearing Gallois' mother's crucifix. It made him realize something that made him feel ashamed. "You know, after all those years at the church, I can't remember ever having one conversation with Father Jacob about religion. He said this was a holy war. I don't know how to fight that kind of war. I am no clergy man. I wasn't even sure I believed in heaven and hell until—"

"Until you saw them," Lisa finished. "But you believe now. Because you saw hell in those things' eyes. But now you're not sure if God will save you because you did not really believe in Him until now." She wrapped an arm around him, and he wasn't sure which of them were trembling. He looked at the crucifix. He realized she must have had a similar conversation with Gallois' mother when she spoke, as though from memory.

"It doesn't matter because we believe now. We have to have faith in him now. That's the hard part."

He did not know what to say that. What she was suggesting was going to take time, and what she and the Knights needed right now was a leader with strong convictions, not questionable ones. "I don't think I'm the right man for this," he finally admitted. "I'm not ready. I thought I was, but I'm not."

Lisa laid her head on his chest. "Dad believed in you and so did Father Jacob."

"Yeah, they did, didn't they?" He pulled away from her, "Now they're gone." He walked toward the door and could not bring himself to look back when she called to him.

0900 Hours

Gallois watched Malcolm from the roof of the Oasis compound. A caravan of military vehicles was driving onto the grounds. The vehicles entered the front gate and were directed into the building through the blast doors. A single jeep stopped outside the blast doors where Malcolm was standing, and a large man climbed out. Gallois assumed the man was the general that Malcolm had been expecting. Malcolm shook hands with the man, and the two of them walked over to the parcel of sand that had been cleared of bodies only an hour ago. They stood there talking for several minutes before walking inside the building.

He hoped Malcolm was telling the man the truth about what he was about to get into. They needed help. He understood that. But it did not seem right to ask for more people to risk their lives. The demons were unnatural. He doubted these normal people could protect them. He glanced over at the outlook window.

Blood was still on the wall below the window frame because it was too high for the firehoses to reach. He decided he would clean it at nightfall. But did it matter? More blood was sure to come. The demons had gotten in there once and taken whatever it was they wanted. There was no reason to believe they could not do it again.

Malcolm had asked him to stay out of sight until he had an opportunity to bring the general to meet him. He imagined the General would try to convince him of their safety. The thought of hearing those words made him angry. It was a lie, one that he felt stupid for having once believed. The truth was, he had never been safe. He understood that last night after his mother told him Father Jacob had been killed.

Now memories were all he had left of Father Jacob. They were fond, vivid memories and most were during from his youth, before the glass walls of his chamber. But the one memory he wanted to recall escaped him. No matter how hard he tried, he could not remember the last good moment they had shared. The only memory to come close was of a short visit three days ago.

Father Jacob had tried to interact with him but he was having a bad morning. He had faked being happy to see him. Seconds before Father Jacob entered, he had released his pet parrot from its cage and let it fly through the window to a freedom that he would never have. He wished he had known that was the last moment they would have alone together. He wished he had sensed it. Why didn't his telepathy warn him? Why must it only warn him of demons?

He sighed, knowing he was making excuses. He could not blame it on his telepathy. He should have told Father Jacob how he felt about him long ago. Now he could never say what he had always felt. He could not tell him that he loved him. All he could do now was say the words in a prayer and hope that Father Jacob heard them.

Tears welled in his eyes. He never thought he could feel worse than he did when he was in that chamber. But he knew now that there was something worse than the feeling of hopelessness, feeling—lost. The police had retrieved Father Jacob's body and brought it onto the grounds per the Vatican's order. He saw what the possessed had done to his protector. Now he understood the cruelty of murder and saw the shell that remain when a soul left a body.

He dreaded the thought of seeing the body of a man who had protected and raised him lying in a box then seeing that box lowered into the ground and disregarded. There had to be a better way of honoring a man who had meant so much. But all his protector would get was a few kind words and flowers. The more he thought about it the more he came to believe death was the worst that could ever happen.

He did not want to be alone right now. He wanted to talk to someone. But whom could he talk to? Lisa was even more of a mess than before. And his mother would only offer words of hope. Optimistic words were the last thing he wanted to hear right now. He would rather hear the truth. Everything was as black and empty as the two holes on Leba's face.

He wiped sweat from his forehead and gazed at the sun and clouds above the horizon. He wondered if that were what heaven looked like. Was Father Jacob seeing something similar? Could he see him right now? He imaged Father Jacob looking down on him from heaven and telling him that he was still there and no longer in pain. He knew he was only imaging what he wanted, but it felt good. Father Jacob spoke to him as he always had, telling him to have faith and not to be afraid.

He tried for Father Jacob and only then could feel the sun on his face and the air in his lungs. He wiped his brow and looked back at the horizon with new eyes. He marveled at the barren space. In most books he had read, the desert was depicted as a harsh, unforgiving place where people were brought to suffer some horrible death before being buried in unmarked graves. The mere site of it represented misery. But that was not his opinion. This land was beautiful: the endless, wavy sand dunes, rugged pillars, the archaic appearance of the Joshua trees, all of it there before him. It felt like forgotten country, and it was open to anyone that would have it, even him.

He closed his eyes and imagined flying over the terrain. He let himself get lost in the thought of open sky and the feel of a cool breeze on his face. When he opened his eyes, he realized he did not have imagine or wish. He wasn't looking through glass. What he wanted was right in front of him.

He stepped up onto the edge of the roof and then unfolded his wings to stretch them wide. Before he could use his wings to thrust himself into the sky, his telepathy beckoned. Without thinking, he turned around, expecting to see his mother or a Knight standing behind him, but there was no one there. He surveyed the area. His eyes were drawn to a spot only ten feet away. He saw only concrete and the corner of an air conditioning unit, but his telepathy insisted that there was something more. He stepped down from the ledge and slowly walked over to the spot. His heartbeat was racing. He kept telling himself that if a demon were present his telepathy would warn him.

When reached the spot, he was too afraid to stretch out a hand. "Who are you?" he asked, in a shaky voice. There was no answer. He raised his voice and asked again, hoping to be laughing about this in a few seconds.

A flash of white light momentarily blinded him. When he opened his eyes, what appeared to be a man was standing before him. He choked on a breath as he stepped backward. He arched his wings, readying himself to fly away, but he waited for the man to make a move. The man was tall and wore a white chiton and brown sandals. His blue eyes were staring down at him, and the weight of them made Gallois's head lower as if he were seeing something he was not supposed to.

Gallois's thoughts were tripping over each other. He was afraid to speak. The man looked at him as if he were expecting something. But when Gallois opened his mouth the man turned away and looked toward the outlook window. Knights were repelling down to clean the remaining blood from the wall.

The man slowly shook his head. "Look at them. They think they can simply undo what has been done." He had a soothing, kind voice that made Gallois a little less afraid. He turned back to Gallois and looked him over. "And you desire to be like them."

Gallois inched closer. His mind was buzzing. He asked the only question that made sense. "Are you an angel?"

The being did not answer. His eyes narrowed just enough for Gallois to notice.

"Why don't you have wings?" Gallois asked.

The man's lip curled. "You see only what we want you to see, Nephilim."

Gallois eyes widened more with the realization of being in the presence of an angel. He wilted, fell to his knees, and started crying so hard it hurt. He had prayed for this moment. He knew, if he kept praying and believing, one day an angel would appear. He tried to speak through his tears. If he could just get the words out, ask the question as it said in the Bible, "Ask and it shall be given unto you."

"Please," he begged, crouching as he inched closer, groveling at the angel's sandaled feet. "Please, make me normal?"

"No."

Stunned, waited for the angel to speak again. The angel reached down and placed a head atop his head. It felt soft and warm as comforting as his mother's touch. He waited for the angel to speak. The angel knelt down, put a hand under his chin to lift his head, and stared into his eyes,

"It's the human side of you that causes you to hate yourself so. It knows that it is corrupt with wickedness and should not exist. Such has happened before, in the time before The Flood. Children like you were born. Their existence brought death to those who loved them and then unto the world." He leaned down even more. "Evil corrupts. Do you think it is coincidence that you can sense them?

Gallois closed his eyes. The angel knew the one secret he had kept buried deep within himself, never saying it aloud. He had never said the words before. But now there was no reason to keep quiet. The words burned his throat when he spoke them. "They never should have had me," he said. "I'm evil."

"No. They should not have," the angel said firmly. "Your father wanted me to believe it was love that made him descend. But it was not. It was lust." He stood upright and turned his back and walked away.

Gallois head hung low. He stared at the concreate floor, thinking at first only of the damning confirmation he had just received. Then he considered the angel's remarks about his parents and felt a twinge of anger as his head rose. The one thing that had always been clear to him was that his parents had loved each other. He looked at the angel with sobering eyes. The angel's long blond hair triggered a memory—which quickly led to more. He was standing in his crib watching his father on the balcony taking to a tall man with long blond hair. "I remember you," he said. The angel turned around and grinned. "You were there the night Dad was taken."

"Yes. I was there," the angel answered. "You watched me and your father from your window as you would everything else shorty after." He chuckled.

"You let them take my father?" he asked.

The angel scoffed. "You would think that wouldn't you Nephilim. I did not let anything happen to him. I accepted what he was willing to let happen." He turned away ignoring Gallois's as his chest rose and fell. "You could never truly understand what I am about to say because your mind has limitations." His brows furled as he turned further away. "Your father was my brother, as it was intended in the beginning. He betrayed that holy love that binds families. He turned his back on me. He turned his back on his family." The angel turned around. "It was not I who wronged your father. He wronged me."

Gallois stood up. His eyes were shining golden yellow. "But you were there. You could have helped him, but you didn't because you were mad at him? What kind of angel are you?" He approached the creature and wondered if this were even an angel at all. "What kind of angel lets demons hurt people? My father was a good man!"

Victor's eyes slowly lit up a slightly whiter yellow color of their own. "You think you know what constitutes a good person? You, a boy who has spent his life cowering in a room and blaming his mommy for it? You only had to ask to be let out that room. But the truth was you were hiding from the evil you saw, that evil that lies within every human. Your father tainted himself with your mother's evil, and he got what he deserved!"

Gallois swung at him. Angelic wings appeared at Victor's back as he caught Gallois's fist with blinding speed. Victor punched him in the chest and the force of the blow sent Gallois flying backwards like a ball struck by a bat. He back smacked against a wall fifteen feet away, and then he landed hard on the concrete.

Gallois's chest was aflame. He raised his head. Victor hadn't moved. The angel's eyes were like blue fire, which only made him angrier. If he had taken a second to think, he would have considered the fact he did not have the advantage in this fight he had with Ramiro and Lisa. Instead, he pushed himself up and charged Victor again.

Victor grabbed him effortlessly by the collar and raised him from the floor. "You dare to smite me?" he demanded, tightening his grasp. "You speck of flesh!"

He tossed Gallois back into the same wall much harder this time, and everything went black.

Chapter 12

A PALE GRAY, hideously emaciated demon ran through the streets on all fours, dodging and weaving through traffic. Tires screeched. Cars swerved and collided with each other. The demon roared and clawed when headlights shone on its elongated face and cast light into the depths of its pitted eyes. The demon kept looking up into the night sky. With a roar, it ran from the street, rounded a corner, and disappeared into the darkness of an alley.

Seconds later, five angels armed with golden swords glided down from the sky and followed the creature on foot. The angles were of different ethnicities and genders, three were male with ebony skin. The other two were female with white and olive skin. Their bodies were lean and muscular. The color of their wings matched their hair. They moved like gladiators as they searched the darkness for the demon, sharing brief glances as they communicated telepathically.

"Looking for someone?" Sean asked, emerging from the darkness, barefoot and wearing metal hand claws on both of his hands wet with blood.

The angels looked at each other again, and then the taller of the ebony-skinned angels stepped out from the others.

"What have you done, Sean?"

Sean smiled, raised his arms, and offered, "I've freed myself from the human condition."

The angel regarded the hand-claws. "No, you have not. You've doomed yourself and many others." The angel's face turned sad. "Sean, why have you used your gift in such a way?"

Sean scoffed, but it sounded more like a hiss. "Gift? All I ever got from this gift was pain!"

The angel slowly shook his head. "You never understood. You were supposed to find purpose in your struggles."

Sean's pale face tightened. His voice was almost childlike. "You weren't born in this world, angel. You don't know what it's like. You've never suffered, never prayed for pain to end." He pointed at the angel as tears welled in his reddened eyes. "I did everything He asked! I did not sin. I lived by the Word. And what did I get? More pain! Well, I'm done asking. Now I've made it so I'll never suffer again. I did that! Not Him!" Sean smiled, but tears fell from his eyes, and he suddenly seemed to have trouble speaking. "And see now?" he asked, grabbing at his chest. "You see how things change? You speak to me now." The rasp in his voice increased, and he was barely intelligible. "You stand before me. Is this what it takes?" He cringed and his body began to shudder to the sounds of bones twisting and snapping. He screamed and fell to the ground. His clothes ripped as his flesh stretched and bulged.

Suddenly, the sounds of demons erupted from all around. The angels pulled their swords from their sheaths and assumed fighting stances. Sean continued to change and scream. His limbs grew, his spine elongated. Within seconds, he appeared more dog than human.

He charged the angels, and suddenly other demons emerged from the darkness like mutated dogs, their claws leaving scratches on the ground. The angels were quickly surrounded and engaged in combat. Both groups moved with unnatural speed, but the angels were more graceful, wilding their swords with deadly accurately. Within two bloody minutes it was clear the demons were outmatched. The demons howled and wailed as the angels' swords sliced and hacked into their muscular bodies with the sound of sizzling flesh and sight of spurting blood.

The certainty of winning the battle was lost when possessed men next appeared from the darkness. The angels continued working as a team using their telepathy. With each passing minute, the ground got slicker and the number of demons and possessed increased.

Suddenly, one of the angels was sliced on the leg by a demon's weapon. The wound was deep and went the full length of the angel's thigh. There was no blood or exposed bone, only a hollow darkness. For a second the angel did not notice the injury. Then, wincing, the angel looked down. The texture of the skin around the wound slowly changed, reddening as bone and tissue appeared and blood began to flow. In seconds, the wound appeared days old and infected. The angel dropped to one knee, and the demons took advantage and killed him. The angel's sword fell from his hand, and its texture changed from gold to bass, and it began to rust away as it lay on the ground.

The lead angel looked in the fallen angel's direction as he ducked under claws. He continued fighting, impaling one demon while using another angel's sword to kill a creature flung in his direction. Minutes passed, and two more angels fell. The leader looked in the direction of the other angels and spread his wings, and they all started flying up toward the open sky.

Demons were waiting on the walls as they ascended and they flung their bodies out, trying to stop the angels' escape. The angels narrowly made it into the sky, but the lead angel only saw three of them. He looked down and saw the fourth angel descending back into the ally from the combined weight of the demons hanging on him.

The lead angel maneuvered and dived back down into the alley just as the angel's body disappeared into the darkness. The other two angels looked on. Suddenly, they heard a demon's scream, and the leader came flying up to them holding the other angel by the arm. The leader released the angel as they joined the others. The four of them hovered, looking down at the alley.

"We will get others," one angel said. The lead angel touched a wound on his face and looked curiously at the blood that came from it.

"No," the lead angel answered. "They are using Descender blood. We will warn the others and develop another strategy."

They flew higher into the sky and disappeared into the clouds.

Chapter 13

MALCOLM LED GENERAL Hinshaw to the infirmary. The Knights had found Gallois unconscious on the roof. He had regained consciousness, and Malcolm was eager to learn what had happened to him. A map of the facility shook in Malcolm's sweaty hands as he studied their path. He tried to steady them, hoping the general hadn't noticed, but he was sure this older, more experienced man had.

He went over a check list in his head. Every precaution he had been trained to take had been taken. If his Knights had missed something, he was going to come down hard on them. After all they'd been through, the last thing they needed was one of those creatures loose in the facility. He led the general down another hallway with a single room at its end. They neared the room and he pondered quick words to summarize Gallois. But no ephemeral words could describe the boy who had challenged everything he understood about life.

And there was no taming his thoughts about Gallois. The boy was something unnatural. The only explanation for him came wrapped in a word that should have brought him ease but it didn't. It scared him. If Gallois were an angel, what did that mean?

He and the general entered the infirmary. The room appeared untouched by the Nesphar. It was enormous and filled with machines, none of which he recognized. He looked across the room and saw a woman wearing a lab coat standing in front of Gallois as he put his shirt back on. Malcolm got a glimpse of two parallel folds of skin on Gallois's back. He realized that was where his wings came from. He wondered if the doctor had discovered that as well.

He and the general reached the bed and saw the woman was holding a penlight up to Gallois face as she tried to persuade him to remove his googles.

"Come on, let me see those pretty eyes," the woman crooned.

Gallois shook his head slowly then put his hands on the sides of his goggles. Malcolm remembered how Gallois's eyes had shone that night and understood his reluctance to oblige the woman. Before he could intervene, the general did.

"Problems, Doc?" the man said with a chuckle. The doctor turned around, and the sight of her made Malcolm feel as though some one were playing a joke on him. The woman smiling back at him could not possibly be a doctor. She looked like one of the models in the photographs at the dentist's office; her teeth were pearly white, her cheeks red, and her skin was glowing.

"Hi, General." the doctor said. "Just looking after my first patient. Um, Gal—"

"Gallois," Malcolm finished. "How is he?"

"He's fine," the doctor said with strange enthusiasm. "He had a small lump on the back of his head, but it's nothing to worry about." She turned and smiled at Gallois. "He's being secretive about how it happened but I'm guessing someone was playing on the roof and had an accident." Gallois lowered his head and, without thinking, Malcolm laid a hand on Gallois's shoulder as he had often seen Ramiro do.

The general chuckled again. "Well, it's OK to get hurt during play. Shows you take your play seriously." The military man offered his hand. "Hello, Gallois. I'm General Hinshaw. It's nice to finally meet you." Gallois took the man's hand and greeted him nervously. Malcolm could tell all the kid wanted was get out of there.

"You've met Doctor Klein," Hinshaw said. "That's assuming she introduced herself before she started examining you. Sometimes she forgets that bedside manner is an important part of the job." He and Dr. Klein exchanged quick, sarcastic smiles before he turned back to Malcolm. "Lieutenant, Doctor Klein will be your CMO. She's top-notch, graduated from medical school before her last permanent tooth came in."

Stands of her blond hair fell on her forehead as she shook his hand. "Pleasure to meet you, Lieutenant. Thanks for having me onboard." Gallois stood up, and Klein stopped him in a way that suggested she'd expected him to try to leave. "Wait a moment, Gallois. Don't worry, we're almost finished here. Just let me talk to Malcom and the general for a second, and we'll finish up, OK?" Gallois sighed and sat back down on the bed.

Klein gestured for Malcom and Hinshaw to follow her before they walked over to an X-ray display.

Klein stared at Malcolm for a second before speaking, and then gave him a cautious eye. "What do you know about this kid?" she asked.

"Not much," he answered. "They'd keep him under lock and key for years. The only person that had access to him was Ramiro." He did not know how much of a lie that was, but he sensed she had learned something about Gallois and he wanted to know what that was.

Klein stared at him again, but she seemed to be convinced he was telling to the truth. The general gave Malcolm a guarded glance while asking, "What is it, Doctor?" Klein flicked a button on the display, and two a very complicated black-and-white imagines appeared.

"These X-rays are of Gallois' chest," Klein said, as if the images spoke for themselves.

Malcolm squinted. "What the hell is all that?"

Klein answered excitedly, "They're feathers." She pointed. "You see these bones here? There are two sets of radii, ulnae, and humeri bones. Now, by themselves they are bones of the arm and forearm. But when you include these smaller bones located here at the ends, you have—."

"Wings," Malcolm finished. There was an ah-ha expression on Dr. Klein's face.

Hinshaw gasped. "What?"

Malcolm sighed. This was not how he wanted this to happen. "I was going to tell you about that before I introduced you to him, General."

Klein scoffed. "Tell him? The whole science community needs to know about this." Malcolm turned to Hinshaw. His face was just as tight as his own because each of them knew the diplomatic consequences of speaking of Gallois or anything associated with the Vatican. The U.S. government had long ago established a nondisclosure agreement with the Vatican.

Hinshaw cleared his throat and gave Dr. Klein a stern eye, to which she reluctantly succumbed. "Please excuse the doctor," Hinshaw said. "She still doesn't quite understand the need for secrecy with what we do. Don't worry, nothing will be disclosed to the public, science or otherwise. And if something should get leaked, that person will find themselves doing time and not on the cover of TIME." The turned an eye past Dr. Klein's now reddened-face, and looked at Gallois with a perplexed stare. "What else did you find out about him, doctor?"

Dr. Klein tapped keys on a nearby computer. "I tested his blood. I couldn't match his blood type to any known genome." She tapped more keys, and two hexagons appeared on the screen. "This is an image of a normal strand of DNA, and here is Gallois'. There are four polymer chains. All four are phosphate and glucose based, but there are other unknown polymers."

Hinshaw frowned, and she continued before he could speak.

"What I'm trying to get you to understand, general General, is that Gallois' physical attributes are unprecedented." She picked up three Polaroids from the table. "When they brought him to me, he had a gash on the back of his head. Ten minutes later, it had completely healed." She turned to Malcolm. "With your permission, I'd like to run more tests on him."

Hinshaw cleared his throat. "You're asking the wrong person. Lieutenant Elton, will be working under my command until further notice. And to answer your question, that decision rests with the boy and his mother. But you can just put all of that out of your mind for now. I want everyone focused on stopping these lunatics."

Hearing mention of Gallois' mother brought to mind a question Malcolm felt needed to be asked. "Does his mother know he's in here?"

"I don't know," Dr. Klein answered.

"She's very protective of him. You should call her."

Hinshaw pulled on his arm and led him back to Gallois. The general was more polite than before. His eyes roamed over the boy and responded to every move and fidget as he divulged more pleasantries. He ended their conversation with an assurance of safety. All the while, his wide eyes looked down at Gallois as if he might suddenly disappear. He watched Gallois' hand in his as he shook it before he said goodbye.

Gallois followed his mother into the Oasis auditorium. The room was crowded with soldiers. They whispered among each other as they stood shoulder to shoulder. The room smelled of shoe polish and canvas surplus. He followed as she nudged a path through the soldiers. He looked in the distance, between the men, and saw a large stage and podium halfway across the room. When they finally reached the foot of the stage, he spotted Lisa standing a few feet away wearing a uniform. He raised his arm trying to get her attention, but there were too many soldiers between them.

He heard a commotion on the right side of the room and turned to see Hinshaw leading Malcolm and other soldiers onto the stage. They stopped and stood next to a large black tarp covering something. Malcolm and the soldiers lined up behind Hinshaw, and the general stepped to the front of the stage,

"All right, listen up! For those of you who don't know me, I'm General Hinshaw, your new commanding officer. I have been sent to help Lieutenant Elton deal with an extremely hostile situation. And believe me when I tell you we're going to neutralize this threat! For you soldiers who arrived with me, Lieutenant Elton and his Knights have an advantage over us. They have seen the enemy. They've seen what we're up against." He took a moment and stared into the crowd then chuckled, "Demons! That's what the people who sent us are calling our adversaries."

He made a gesture, and two soldiers pulled away the tarp to reveal two corpses of possessed men who had attacked Oasis. The soldiers gasped at the sight of the burnt, bullet- riddled corpses lying before them with monstrous elongated limbs, bloody eye sockets, and open mouths.

Hinshaw continued. "I think, demon is an appropriate name for these things because when they're killed, their bodies burn. As you can see, these two demons died from rifle fire."

Hinshaw continued. "I think 'demon' is an appropriate name for these things because, when they're killed, their bodies burn. As you can see, these two demons died from rifle fire."

He knelt down beside one of the corpses. "The soldiers who killed these demons used M-16s. Normally, a few rounds in the chest would be enough to kill any man, but these things are able to sustain a lot more damage. Lieutenant Elton's men emptied entire clips into these things, and they kept coming. For that reason I am equipping all of you with more powerful firearms."

He stood up. "The enemy will look like civilians. They're freakishly fast, so avoid hand-to-hand combat with them."

A soldier yelled from the crowed, "Sir! If they look like civilians, how do we identify them?"

"Well, just look at them Soldier. They're supremely ugly. I don't think you'd confuse something like this as normal. But for those of you who're used to looking at ugly things, the enemy can be most easily identified by these exaggerated limbs and a pungent odor of sulfur. So once we reach the city and began checking locations, beware of any facility with the smell. And if you're still unsure as to whether or not he or she is the enemy, take the necessary precautions until you are sure." He looked down at Gallois. "Come here, Son."

Feeling hot with nervousness, Gallois walked from his mother's side and climbed the steps to the podium and soon felt Hinshaw's hand on his shoulder.

Gallois tried to gather the nerve to look out into the audience but fear only allowed sight of those closest to the podium including his mother, who looked on with a bewildered stare.

Hinshaw nodded at Gallois, and he exposed his wings and spread them wide. The crowd gasped.

Hinshaw waited a moment before speaking. "Now, I'm not sure where you are in regards to religion or whether or not you believe in spiritual beings at all. But I want you to approach these things as if they are demons because I have experienced enough in life to know the devil does exist!"

"Sir, is that an angel?" a soldier asked from the crowd.

The crowd was pin-drop silent.

Hinshaw looked at Gallois. Gallois hoped Hinshaw would not say yes. He had convinced Gallois to show his wings as a way of inspiring the soldiers, but he had promised not to say he was an angel. Gallois's heart raced, seeing now how easy it would be for Hinshaw not to honor his word.

"This young man's name is Gallois," the general said. "Gallois is a friend, and he's agreed to help us. He and I both believe the enemy would like to harm him, and he has courageously offered to help us take advantage of that by allowing us to use him as bait."

As Hinshaw continued, Gallois saw his mother was pushing her way closer to the stage.

The general rested his hands on his hips. "I've assured Gallois that he need not worry about being harmed because we're going to protect him to the fullest!" He turned back to the crowd. "With all I've shared with you this evening, I know what some of you are thinking right now. Hell, this all might seem frightening to most."

He walked to the edge of the stage. "But some of you are like me, happy with the idea that these creatures are demons! Do you know why? Because Satan has been a pain in my ass for a long time! I'm happy for an opportunity to return the favor! I'm ready to inflict fifty-seven years of anger on him!"

The soldiers began to cheer and shout "Bravadoes!"

Excitement began to infiltrate the room.

Hinshaw clinched his fist. "I had to endure years of corruption, hate, and murder. I've seen Satan use this tools to destroy those I love and my fellow man. I think it's about time he and I met one on one!"

He took a M16 from one of the soldiers and raised it above his head. "I've got something I'd like to give him for all his hard work!"

The room began to rumble as Hinshaw continued,

"But even with my power, I can't send this message alone! I need help. But not help from just anyone. I need someone who's willing to go through hell and back just to make a point! I need a Marine!"

The cheering swelled to a deafening uproar.

Hinshaw smiled wickedly. "Oh, you guys sound livid! I believe I'm in the presence of Marines! Well, let's go show these demons what hell really is! Hoo-rah!"

The soldiers joined him in unison. "Hoorah!"

--*▦◎ ◎▦*--

Smack! Heather's hand landed hard against the side of Malcolm's face. Gallois eyes widened. He reached for her, but stopped after she threw up her hand.

Her head jerked back and to stare at Malcolm. "Are you crazy? You're going to get him killed!"

Hinshaw stepped between them, slightly raising his hands. "Ms. Gavreel, Malcolm didn't have anything to do with this. It was your son who volunteered for this."

"And you listened to a fifteen-year-old?"

"Ms. Gavreel, under the circumstances, we have very few options, and our window of opportunity is limited. There's more chance of these creatures showing themselves if your son is there."

"So what you're telling me is that your need to hurry is worth risking my son's life".

Malcolm was rubbing his face. "Heather, the Nesphar took Ian so they could force him to open a gateway to hell."

Malcolm's words silenced her for only a moment. "What are you talking about? Father Jacob said that, all the people who knew about that had died."

"Yeah, I know. That's what he and the Vatican thought. But no secret like that every dies. The Vatican is sure the Nesphar have found it. That's the only reason they'd be interested in Ian."

Hinshaw interrupted, "Therefore, the Nesphar are no longer our primary concern. If a gateway has been opened, more powerful demons will be released. The longer it stays open, the harder it will be to fix the damage."

"How do you know all this?" she asked.

"I've been helping the Vatican for years," Hinshaw said. "I assure you, Gallois will be well protected." He turned to Gallois and said, "We'll give you two time to talk. If you're still interested in helping us, we'll be waiting in the conference room."

The air did not seem to move as Gallois watched Malcolm and the soldiers follow Hinshaw off the platform. He had hoped one of them would stay nearby, but no such luck. The last of the soldiers exited through the door and closed it behind him.

His mother rolled her eyes at the closed door. "I hope he doesn't think that I won't be calling the Vatican myself. If Father Jacob weren't sure he would have told me."

"It's true Mom," Gallois said.

"How do you know?" she snapped. "You can't trust either of them."

Gallois did not answer at first. "Mom, I have to help them. I am going to help them."

Heather's blinked her eyes then challenged. "Really? Even if I say don't?"

"Yes." He answered in a near whisper.

Heather looked him full on the face. "Have you thought this through? What if something happens? You can't depend on that General. He only cares about his mission. You'll come second."

"This is more important than me, Mom." His forehead creased as he looked at the floor. "And if we win, you and I won't have to hide anymore."

"Gallois, this isn't about winning. This is about surviving. I don't care about the hiding. All I care about is that we are to-gether and safe. That's enough. That's all anyone could ask for."

"No, it's not!"

Heather stared at him for several seconds. There were a lot of things he could say to her right now: how sick he was of living in a single room. How every day he wished he had never been born. How he would rather die than go back to living in a chamber.

But his mother did not say anything. Yet in the silence he believed she understood how he felt. Maybe she always had.

His mother's eyes swelled as she gripped her crucifix tightly with her shaking hands. "As a mother, I can't give you permission to do this. I just can't. But I will accept your decision. I won't try to stop you."

He was surprised. He had not expected her to agree so easily or soon. It was the first time he had ever challenged her authority and her having yielded left him with mixed feelings of accomplishment and shame. He did not know how to respond. He tried to think of something fitting to say, but nothing special came to mind so he spoke the only words that did come to mind. "Thank you."

He turned to leave, and his mother pulled him into a tight hug that left him knowing how difficult it was for her to allow this. After a few seconds, she gently pushed him away, and, feeling even more ashamed, he walked from the podium and exited the auditorium without looking back.

Chapter 14

THE LAS VEGAS lights shined brightly on the horizon as the small caravan of military vehicles made its way to the city. Gallois sat in the rear of an armored transport van, waiting for General Hinshaw to give word for him to fly ahead to a location in the city. In his hand was an aerial photo of an alley Hinshaw had given him. He studied the photo for the eighth time to direct his eyes away from the soldiers watching him. There were ten of them in the vehicle, setting poker-faced as they cradling their rifles. Their eyes had not often left Gallois's direction since he had entered the van.

It was a long ride, probably longer for the soldiers because he had the advantage of being able to hide behind his tinted goggles. That was the only good thing about them. The soldiers had no way of knowing that his eyes had been closed most of the ride, his way of attaining privacy. And he needed it. He used it to give himself a pep talks. I am not going to die. Don't be scared. I am not alone. But that approach did not work as well as he would have liked. He kept remembering demonic nightmares. His ability to see people's inner demon made night terrors uniquely frightening for him.

He looked at the front of the transport vehicle where Lisa was in the passenger's seat. When they bordered the vehicle, his insecurities had gotten the best of him. He sat away from her, not waiting to appear as if he needed a babysitter to the older male soldiers. He soon regretted it when he found himself setting alone. Ironically, the soldiers sat together and comforted each other with random chest slaps and proclaiming bad intentions for what they were calling the "funk monsters". None of their comforting trickled down to him so, instead of feeling like man he felt isolated.

Lisa turned in her seat, stood, and started in his direction. She was holding a radio. As she walked, Hinshaw's voice sounded over the radio. "Ok, we're a few miles from the city. Send him out. Make sure the tracker is fixed securely!"

"Copy," Lisa answered in a soldierly tone that sounded like the one she used to make fun of her dad. She gestured for him to stand up. When he did, she quickly checked the tracking device and communicator attached to the underside of his collar. She sounded worried when she said, "You can just speak normally, and we'll hear you. Are you ready?"

"Yes." he answered, feeling anything but as he removed his goggles.

She grabbed his shoulders. "You be careful, Ok?" she said, sounding more like the Lisa he knew. In her worried eyes, he saw something more than the glow of his eyes. He saw the years they had shared together and the love she felt for him. He hoped she could see the same in his.

"I will." he said.

She told him to be careful again, and hugged him tighter than she ever had before. When she let go, she wiped her eyes and backed away from him.

"OK. Open it," she said, and then there was the pop of an air pressure change followed by a whirling sound as the hatch above slowly opened.

He turned his head upward and saw stars passing above. He drew in a breath and unfolded his wings. The Knights began shouting words of encouragement. His heart raced with excitement. He looked at each soldiers' face and saw nothing but support. He could not fail them. And he wouldn't. Not if he could help it. He gave the Knights a nod, and then arched his back, spread his wings, and used them to thrust through the hatch and into the air. The light coming from the hatch and vehicles' headlights dimmed below as the sky welcomed him. He leveled out and soared toward the city.

Gallois glided around skyscrapers, being sure to stay high and out of the view of the pedestrians below. Most of the office windows he passed were void of light. The moonlight provided enough illumination to cast his reflection on the passing windows. He kept a close eye on the windows fearing that, if he looked away, there would be a demon there when he looked again. He expected his telepathy to give its cold warning at any moment. He glided around the last of the skyscrapers and recognized a cluster of buildings from the aerial photo.

"Gallois, can you hear me?" Hinshaw's deep, boisterous voice sounded from Gallois's communicator.

"Yes. I hear you."

"Your tracking device reads that you're near the targeted location. Do you see it?"

"Yes. I see it."

"Let me know if you see anything. Remember, do not engage them. We just need to know they are in the area. Once you've made visual confirmation, get out of there. We'll set a parameter, close them in and eliminate them."

"Copy, sir," he answered, trying to sound soldierly. He peered down at the darkest part of the alley, and his skin crawled. It felt like something was watching him. His telepathy had not warned him. Maybe this one time when he wanted it to work for him, it wouldn't a fitting revenge for all the years of resentment.

He gathered his nerve. He could not fail. Everyone was counting on him. He maneuvered down into the darkest area between two buildings and then dropped down into the equally dark alley. His apprehensiveness intensified as his shoes touched concrete. The darkness surrounding him felt wet and sticky like fog. The air reeked of sulfur, garbage, and some other odor he could not place.

After walking a few yards, he smelled the unknown scent as strongly as the sulfur. The feeling of something slippery beneath his feet made him stop. Looking down, under the glow of moonlight he saw the blood; it was all over his shoes. He squinted in the darkness and saw more patches of blood scattered on the pavement ahead. His heart had already moved from his chest to his throat, and no matter how hard he tried, he could not swallow.

He squinted hard, as he surveyed the darkness. Luckily, he did not see any bodies. If he could, he probably would not have been able to get his legs moving again. He walked slower, almost tip-toeing through the slick beneath his shoes. Ten feet away, he saw something glimmering on the ground. He walked over, reached down, and lifted the object. It was an old, rusted brass sword, and it was nearly identical to his father's.

"They were here," he whispered. He looked around but no one was there and there was nothing else to find.

They wanted us to find this. He fumbled with his belt, trying to use it to secure the sword when something rattled behind him. His head swung around so fast it hurt, only to find rats sifting through trash outside one of the garbage bins. Beyond the trash bin, he saw the sidewalk and street lamps. People were passing by, unaware of him or the blood.

A cold shiver raced down his back.

A raspy voice sounded from darkest corner of the alley,

"They sent you? How disappointing."

He turned and saw a man standing only thirty feet from him. The man exited the darkness with a labored walk. His skin hung loosely over his bones like oversized clothing, most noticeably below the two gaping holes where his eyes should have been. The only piece of clothing were cream pants stained with dirt and what appeared to be blood.

Gallois stepped backwards took a loose fighting stance. He studied the man's face, and used his telepathy to look pass the empty pits that made him feel as though he were looking at death itself.

Strangely, he did not see an inner soul, only the creature before him.

"Come forth thee to return us to darkness?" Sean cackled. "Well, you're much too late for that, half-breed. This world belongs to us now!"

"Who are you?" Gallois asked, biding time for the Knights.

The man inched closer as he spoke. "I'm he who corrupts man's soul and feeds him sin."

Gallois arched his wings and stepped backwards.

The man hissed. "You're right to fear me, half-breed! I have killed far greater men than you."

"I don't fear you."

"Then you are a fool! Like your father." The man grinned. "He knew fear before he died. And you should know, his last thoughts were of you. He regretted having you."

Gallois stepped forward. "The devil is a liar, and so are you."

The man responded with a deathlike stare and throated growl. Then he said, "fides mortem discens."

Gallois knew the words were Latin. The translation was, faith learns of death.

The man shuddered then his skin stretched then tore, and a bloody mass of pink skin beneath expanded out and overcame his old flesh. Demonic roars erupted from the darkness around him. He looked up to find demonic shadows on the fire escapes blocking his path to the sky. The man's bones cracked and popped as he continued to transform. His skin turned gray, and bat wings tore from his back as he had grew four feet taller.

Gallois glanced over his shoulder to where he had entered the alley, which was now crowded with at least thirty possessed men. He could hear their labored breathing, but they were just standing there. He turned back to the creature the man had morphed into. Even if the Knights arrived at this moment, they would not be able to get to him. Suddenly, Leba jumped down from a railing next to the creature. He wore bloodstained brass knuckles on his hands. The creature snapped its fangs, and Leba cowered away.

The creature charged at Gallois on all fours; the ground trembled with its enormous bulk. It neared, baring its fangs, and Gallois felt as if he were shrinking. He landed an overhand punch to his head, but it had no effect. He felt the air leave his lungs, and he found himself on the ground with fire burning in his chest. The creature grabbed his leg; he kicked it away and used his wings to push himself from the pavement.

After a quick feint, he managed to land a right cross to creature's chin. Its head turned slightly, then returned and smashed into his nose. The creature then clubbed him over the head, sending him face- first down to the pavement. The alley was spinning as he struggled to his feet. He felt the creature's monstrous hand engulf his neck and then his feet leave the ground as the pressure of the chokehold intensified. He stared into the face of the creature holding him. Red began to bleed into the image. He was holding the creature's forearms. Judging by the pressure of the grip, there was no prying the hand away. He desperately searched his waistline for the angelic sword as the world grew darker. His hand found the sword, and its rusted edge was still sharp enough to cut through his belt as he pulled it free and stabbed the creature in the stomach.

The creature roared and dropped him. The blade did not cut deeply, only about four inches, but it was enough. He grabbed the blade. Gallois pushed up from his knees and used both hands to thrust it deeper. But the blade was too dull and would not cut farther. The creature knocked him away, and he fell, taking the sword with him. When he looked up, the creature was retreating into the darkness, and two demons were dropping down from above. They roared and snarled as they charged at him, barring fangs and scraping the pavement with their claws. He pushed to his feet and readied the rusty sword.

The demons attacked with blinding speed and furiously. It took all of his unnatural speed to avoid them. He dodged and swung, adjusting his wings to match his movements as to not have them grabbed. For the first time in his life, he did not hold anything back. He hit the creatures so hard, he could feel their bones fracture, swung the rusty sword so fast it seemed sharp. But the demons never stopped even with broken bones and hanging flesh and it was a reminder that it was only a matter of time. He kept looking for a quick exit but every escape was blocked.

The two demons paced around him as the possessed men moved in closer, leaving at little less distance for him. He looked at the rusted sword. It had broken twice and now too short to be of any real use. A smirk lined on both of the demons hideous faces. They charged then separated one demon scaled the wall. The other moved farther to the left. The demon on the wall leaped from the wall and was overhead. Gallois used his wings to catch the creature in the air. Their bodies collided in the air then smacked on the pavement. The demons was on top of him and was impossible to remove. They scuffled as the other demon moved in.

He brought the broken sword to bear and stuck its end into the demon's throat. Blood rained down on him before the demon choked on its own fluid and fell aside. Before he could get up, the second demon tackled him. He increased his effort to free himself of the demon, but it was clear he was not going to be able to in time. When the possessed reached them, he screamed, as his legs and arms came alive with piercing from their biting.

An explosion near the possessed people at the entrance, sent bodies flying through the air. The sound of automatic gunfire followed. The possessed scattered, and he caught a glimpse of the Knights moving into the alley. He took advantage of the confusion and crawled away.

Demons began dropping down from the fire escapes and following the possessed as they ran in the direction of gunfire. For a moment, he thought they had forgotten about him. Then he felt something fall on him. It was Leba, trying to rip the skin from his face with his metal claws. Gallois thrust out his wings, taking both of them into the air.

He rose higher and higher, hoping the threat of falling would cause Leba to flee. But Leba was undeterred and tried to claw his neck, seemingly content to fall tc their mutual deaths if it meant their mutual destruction.

Gallois continued to rise. Soon they were well beyond the rooftops. He managed to grab one of Leba's arms and used it to shake him from his back. The last he saw of Leba was his boney face as it fell into the darkness. Gallois inhaled deeply, exhausted, hurt, and bleeding. He looked below and saw orange streaks of gunfire coming from beyond the transport vans. He was preparing to fly down to the vehicles when he heard a flapping noise. He looked down and saw the creature flying up after him.

He had barely survived the first encounter with the creature. He did not want a second. He sped off into the city and the creature followed. It did not take long for Gallois to realize how hurt he was. Everything hurt and burned and not even the cold air lessened the pain. In seconds the creature was at his heels. He flew low, dodging around close objects and hoping the creature would crash. But the more he tried the more difficult it was for him as well. Without warning, he got lucky, and the creature crashed into a billboard.

He looked over his shoulder, but the creature was still pursuing. He banked left and rounded a skyscraper. The creature was closing in. Throwing caution to the wind, he flew lower, within full view of the public, trying to lose the creature in oncoming traffic. Pedestrians ducked and screamed as they flew just above head level. The creature was still gaining. It reached for his foot, and he evaded by spiraling upward.

It became obvious that trying to out-fly Mermon was useless. He had only one option, and it was sure to end with him dead. But he had no choice; it was either that or fly until he had mothering left to fight with. He flew lower, searching for a spot advantageous to his smaller frame. But he ran out of time. The creature grabbed him by the ankle and pulled hard. He lost control, grazed a tree limb, and collided with the creature.

They fell from the sky and tumbled to the ground. He was lucky and landed in a grassy area alongside a playground. The creature landed in the street and lost skin as he tumbled then crashed into the tail end of a convertible, arousing the anger of a four heavily tattooed man.

Gallois moved slowly on the ground. His body felt heavy. He heard a scream and lifted his head to find a woman staring at him. She pointed, and more tattooed men appeared. They were all armed with handguns, and they had them aimed at him.

He tried not to look directly at them, his eyes would surely make them shoot. He squinted looking beyond them at the creature, hoping it was dead. The sound of screams told him was alive. Broken glass fell as the creature pulled its bulk up from the vehicle. The tattooed men looked on wide-eyed and shaking with their guns raised but they did not shoot, not even as the creature approached.

Gallois wanted them to shoot but he doubt the handguns would do any damage. And the creature would kill them for it. It might kill them anyway if they did not move aside. With that thought, he knew he needed to get up. He shouted as loudly as he could.

"No! Don't!" he warned the gangsters. "Stay away from it."

The men looked at him with almost equal apprehension, waving their guns from him to the creature.

When he tried to stand, his right knee buckled, and he fell down again. When he was able to get to his feet again, he gestured for the gangsters to move aside and limped toward Mermon.

In the creature's eyes was nothing but bad intentions. He drew in a breath as it approached. When the creature swung at him, he dodged and delivered a side-kick to the creature's back and made it stumble forward. He used the momentum to ram the creature's head into the driver's side window of a car. The creature's massive head was stuck in the ragged glass. Gallois kicked his legs away, causing glass to tear into his neck. Repeatedly, he punched the creature in the ribs. He wished he had something sharp. He wished he had an ax.

The creature flapped one of its wings and knocked him backward. Before he could recover, it had ripped the door from the vehicle and freed itself. It tried to smash Gallois with the door. Gallois stopped it with his foot and punched the creature square on the chin.

The creature recovered and faked an attack with the brass knuckles before landing a blow with the door. After the re-sounding thud Gallois flew backwards and lay sprawled on the ground.

The creature tried again to crush him with the door, but Gallois managed to put his hands up just in time. The creature pressed down on the door with both hands, putting the full weight of its body behind it. With a crash, the creature punched through the door, just missing Gallois' face.

With a frustrated roar, the creature stood up and pulled its arm free of the door, taking a swing at Gallois with the brass knuckles as he tried to stand up. Gallois caught its arm just inches from his face. The sharp edges of the creature's brass knuckles were right in front of his eyes.

As they struggled, a vision flashed through Gallois's mind. In a vast, cave like dwelling, thousands of people were screaming in pain and begging for mercy. Giant demons were torturing them with various piecing weapons. Gallois could feel their emotions: nothing but absolute hopelessness and pain. He tried to shake the image away, but it flashed again; this time clearer. He realized he was seeing people being tortured in hell.

He looked at the hand that he was using to hold back the creature. His glove had fallen off. He was absorbing the creature's memories. The visions intensified. He wanted to release his grip, but if he did he would be struck.

The creature's other hand moved suddenly, and he screamed from the sensation in his chest. It had used his other hand to cut him. The pain was intense and seemed to drain his strength. He managed to force the creature's hand away and move to the side. He looked down at the wound. It was a long gash and it became infected right before his eyes, taking his strength in the process, He fell to his knees.

He was dying.

The creature stood over him. It raised its clawed first, snarling, "Say hello to you father!"

Enraged, Gallois screamed as he used his wings to push himself from the ground. He struck the creature hard with a rising punch. Mermon fell back to the ground, and Gallois followed to land beside him. It was all he had left but not enough to kill.

The creature growled and grabbed him up by the throat. "Die, half-breed!"

The men finally had mustered their courage, and with several loud pops the creature was struck in the back with numerous bullets. It stumbled from the impacts then swung around angrily. The men fired rounds at its head, and after four rounds landed, it flew away off into the night.

Once they were sure the creature was gone, the tattooed men returned their attention to Gallois. He had not moved. They surrounded him. He stared at their guns then closed his eyes, waiting for the sound, the pain, and the unknown.

"Are you okay?" one of the men asked.

Gallois moved slowly but was too weak to speak. Some of the bigger men helped him to his feet, being overly careful not to step on his wings. They gasped when they saw the wound on Gallois' chest that had taken on an infected appearance.

"Gallois?" a girl called, holding out her hand.

Feeling a shift of pressure, he raised his head surprised to hear his name.

The girl was holding his communicator. "They've been calling for you," she said timidly.

He took the communicator from her and held it to his ear.

"Gallois, come in!" It was Lisa. He was happy to hear her voice. They must have killed the demons.

"I'm here."

"Gallois? Where are you? We can't get a clear signal on your position."

Gallois checked the tracking device and found that it was damaged.

"I don't know," he answered.

Another gangster spoke up, "Where are they?"

"Who is that?" Lisa asked.

Gallois looked at the gangster. "A friend. Where are you?"

"We're on Franklin Street, turning in front of a building with red neon lights around it."

"Hey, yo! They at the Denmark building!"

"Which way is it?" Gallois asked.

"About ten blocks that way." The man pointed. "Um south."

"I heard him, Gallois," Lisa said. "We're on our way. Meet us, okay?"

"Okay," Gallois said, placing the communicator in his pocket. He tried to walk, cringing because of the wound on his chest. The stumbled, and the men helped him back upright. He took a few more steps then slowly spread his wings as the small crowd looked on, mystified. "Thank you," he said, taking a last look. With that, he slowly, flew into the night.

Chapter 15

LISA SEARCHED THE sky for Gallois while sitting in the passenger seat of the transport vehicle. She wiped blood from her neck and found a dry spot on her pants to rub her hands on. She and the Marines had cleared the alley of the possessed. The creatures had not seemed as unstoppable as before. It was supposed to be a battle, but it felt more like a slaughter. Within minutes, the creatures were trying to escape. But there was no escaping the massacre; the surrounding buildings had nearly been brought down to make sure of that.

The creatures had been torn apart. And she and her team made sure there weren't any survivors during a final walk through. She had felt nothing but hate when she looked down at the helpless creatures before pulling the trigger. But now, despite the anger still burning within her, she was asking herself questions about the creatures that made her feel guilty.

She looked at her reflection in the window and did not recognize the eyes of the girl staring back at her. The girl her father knew would have never walked into that alley. She knew that girl was gone now. The only piece left of her was in the heart of her friend who was trying to find his way back to her. They had driven several miles away from the alley, and she was relieved. Gallois must have flown away from the danger like she told him to.

She spotted a winged figure in the sky.

"Over there! I see him." she yelled jumping up from her seat to grab a radio from the dashboard. "We're straight ahead of you, Gallois!" She reached over and flashed the vehicle's high beams. "Can you see us?"

She heard Gallois voice, but it quickly faded away.

She continued watching him and saw he was bobbing and losing altitude.

"He's hurt!" she gasped, "Go! Go!"

The driver of the van slammed down on the gas pedal, and the vehicle sped up. She turned to a Knight sitting behind her and ordered, "Tell the medic to get ready." She turned back to the window and saw Gallois falling from the sky to land on the street in front of them. The driver slammed on the brakes, and she bolted from the van with its headlights lighting her way.

He was lying face down, motionless. She slid down beside him, rolled him over, and barely recognized her friend's face. He had been severely beaten. There was so much blood that she did not know where it was safe to touch him. He was unconscious, and she could not wake him. She did all she could do and screamed.

Not long after, Lisa stood at the infirmary room window watching Doctor Klein dressing Gallois' wounds. His face was covered with scratches and bruises; his left eye was swollen shut. His equally injured arms lay at his sides, outside the white bed sheets and below his wings, which were spread wide on the bed the doctor had modified for him. His mother was nearby sitting in a chair reading to him from her bible.

She wished his mother would not read to him that way because it reminded her of funerals. She knew Malcolm was waiting for the right time to bury Father Jacob. She did not want the image of having to bury Gallois too. She watched his mother wipe his forehead and realized that lying on that bed was not just her friend but all that this woman had in this world. If he died, then all the years of hiding and Fabian's death would be for nothing.

Kline dropped bloody swabs into a disposal container and walked over to her.

"How's he doing?" Lisa asked.

She shook her head. "No change."

"What happened to him?"

"I'm not sure." She glanced down at her clipboard. "It's difficult to treat him. I'm still trying to figure out the basics. He has an abnormal blood type. Hell, it's not even on record. That makes it impossible for me to medicate him. I have no reference of safe medications or dosages. Luckily he's healing fast."

"Then you think he'll wake soon?"

"Hard to say. He's in some sort of coma.

The electroencephalogram is showing some unusual brain waves."

"Electro—what?"

"An EEG is a brain scanner. Basically, it measures brain activity. For instance, if the patient is brain dead the scanner shows flat lines, wavy lines for NRE sleep or the first stages of sleep. Typically, the longer we sleep the more active our minds become; this is shown by spiking lines." She unfolded a long narrow, sheet of paper filled with spiking lines. "You don't have to be a med grad to see that this isn't normal. I've been getting this same readout since I hooked it up to him. At first I thought the machine was broken. I had it checked, it's not. For some reason his mind is under a lot of stress. I've got to find a way to get him down to a normal reading."

"If you don't, what will happen?"

Klein looked back through the window. "He's different, but he's still human. There's only so much the mind can take."

Lisa turned away from the doctor and looked back at Gallois. She did not want to think of living without him. Her eyes trailed to Gallois' hands. "He wasn't wearing his gloves," she whispered.

"What?"

"He wasn't wearing one of his gloves when we found him." She looked back at the doctor. "He absorbs memories. He's seeing what those demons have seen."

"I don't understand. Demons? "

Klein stared at her. She could not believe no one had told Klein about what was going on. She did not want to be the one with the difficult task of explaining it to her. Besides, it would not help Gallois get better.

Klein put her hands in her pocket and turned back to the window. "After seeing those corpses you brought back from your mission, I can see why you call them demons."

They saw Gallois' mother suddenly stand up and hurried into the room.

"What's wrong?" Klein asked.

Heather rubbed Gallois' stubbled cheek. "His face—look."

Heather and Klein were probably thinking the same thing she was as they stared down at Gallois. "What's happening to him?" she asked.

Klein was lost in thought, "I don't know." She shuffled through the brain scan readout; it was still full of spiking lines. "Seems like some form of Progeria. The stress on his mind, I think it's aging him."

"Can't you stop it?" Heather asked, now holding her son's hand.

"Believe me. I'm working on it."

"Doctor," General Hinshaw called, standing at the door and well out of Heather's line of sight

Klein pulled herself away from Gallois' bedside and went to him. Lisa watched as they walked further into the hall and then out of view. She told Heather she would return and excused herself. She overheard Hinshaw asking Klein about what she had found when she came around the corner and assumed he was referring to the possessed bodies they had brought back to the site. Klein's face was puzzled, probably wondering why the general was so interested in a bunch of dead bodies, as was she. Klein glanced back at Gallois' room and then brushed a strand of hair from her face. "Follow me," she said.

Hinshaw looked at her as Klein walked. She could see him deciding whether to allow her to follow. He moved his head in the direction of the doctor, and she followed along.

After passing several rooms, they came to a door with an electronic lock. Klein pulled a keycard from her pocket and slid it through the lockbox. The door chimed and slid open and they walked into a very, cold room that made her teeth chatter within seconds. Only Klein was fortunate enough to have her lab coat to guard against the cold.

Lisa forgot about the cold when she saw the demon corpses lying on tables. Rigor mortis had long set in, locking the bodies in unsettled positions. Not even the sting of cold could keep her eyes from widening as she stared down at their demonic eyes and fangs. Her heart raced as ambush scenarios ran through her head. She stood close to Hinshaw, but even he seemed uneasy.

Klein walked over and stood over the closest corpse, "These things, or demons as you'll call them, are some sort of genetically altered humans." She moved her hand along the demon's jawline. "Their bone structure is identical to ours, only—"

"Doctor, I just need to know how to kill 'em."

Klein gave the general an exasperated look. "What you're doing seems to be working."

Hinshaw pointed at one of the corpses. There were at least five holes in the creature's head a dozen more in its chest. "It took all of this just to put this thing down. We needed to know why and how to do it faster."

Klein looked at the creature with new eyes. "I can't give you an exact cause of death," she said." With the caliber of weapons you use, most of these wounds should be fatal. I took out thirty-five bullets from this guy and eighty-three from the other one." She reached into the creature's chest cavity and moved two organs around that appeared identical except for the bullet holes. "Truthfully, these things should have died long before that. I have not found a reason to explain why they didn't."

The door chimed, and Malcolm walked into the room. Before turning to Hinshaw, he looked at Klein and then at her in a way that suggested she should not be there.

"The doctor hasn't come up with anything yet," Hinshaw told him. "For now, we'll just keep shooting the hell out of them."

"You mean there're more of these things?" Klein asked.

"Yes, four that we know of," Malcolm answered. He handed Hinshaw some papers.

"What's this?"

Malcolm pointed to a page. "This building is owned by someone named Oliver Kravis. He worked for Sean ten years ago. His bank account showed a large deposit of two million dollars, and then two days later, more than half of it was withdrawn to purchase this building in Las Vegas two days later. It used to be a health clinic."

"So it was made to house medical equipment," Hinshaw muttered, scanning the paper again.

"There's something else. It has a storage room in the basement. A construction company was working down there just two weeks ago. The police received noise complaints."

Hinshaw rubbed his goatee. "Hmm, good work. Let's check it out."

He and Malcolm walked from the room and Klein hurried behind them. Hinshaw stopped when he noticed they were following.

"How's the boy, Doctor?" he asked.

"He's still unconscious. I've been unsuccessful in finding an adequate—"

"I'm sure you will find a solution. If you need anything, let my men know," the general said dismissively. He turned and continued down the hall with Malcolm, who did not say goodbye.

Lisa watched them leave and could not help but feel left out. When her father was in charge he had told her everything. She looked at Klein, who only shrugged and hurried back into Gallois' room.

Malcolm walked with Hinshaw, not listening to the general after hearing him ask about Gallois. It seemed obvious that Hinshaw was not concerned about the young man. Before that moment he had held the general in high regard. He had thought the general's indifference at times was a way of staying on task.

Shame flushed over him. Until recently, he had not thought much about Gallois either. He shook his head. He did not need a bout with guilt right now. Hinshaw's slightly raised voice redirected his attention.

"Malcolm, we need to hit them hard and kill all those damned things in one shot. And if that gateway is there, we close it for good. I'm not trying to have this situation drawn out into a war."

They turned a corner and came to a briefing room where a tall, thin man sat at the receptionist desk.

"Greg, get us some coffee will you?" Hinshaw asked.

Greg nodded as they entered the room. Malcolm noted the large satellite photograph of the city on the wall.

Hinshaw sat on the edge of the large square table. "Where is this building?" he asked. "And please tell me it's not in some crowded area."

Malcolm went to the photo and used a marker tip to circle a dark-colored building about a quarter of a mile away from the larger buildings. "The building is outside the city."

"Good. Have some men check it out, see if they spot any movement."

"I have. They're already in route."

"OK. If they're there, I want to concentrate all our resources on it."

Malcolm studied the satellite photo. "Are you sure you want to do that? I mean, we've underestimated the Nesphar once before with an assault. What if they've anticipated this already? What if they wanted us to find all this?"

Hinshaw's attention was on Greg as the tall man entered carrying two cups of coffee. He handed a cup to Hinshaw and placed the other on the table before him.

Hinshaw took a sip of coffee and bit out, "That's why we're sending the men to check it out." he said a bit sarcastically.

Malcolm shook his head. "General, if we go in there and it's another ambush, the Nesphar will make sure no one survives."

Hinshaw sucked his teeth. "Lieutenant, don't assume I'm going to make the same mistake as your last commander."

Malcolm slammed his fist on the table. The vibration caused Hinshaw's coffee to spill onto the floor. "What happened was no mistake! Ramiro handled the situation to the best of his ability. I could only hope to become half the man he was!"

Hinshaw glared at him. "Soldier, you're dangerously close to being reprimanded."

Malcolm's expression did not change.

Hinshaw stood and placed his hands on his hips. "Sit down, lieutenant."

Malcolm didn't move.

"Soldier, I said sit down!"

Malcolm sat down.

"You'll have to excuse my flawed people skills. I didn't mean to imply that what happened was due to carelessness. I read Ramiro's file. I know he was an excellent soldier, and I am sure he was good man." He picked up the coffee cup and placed it back on the table. "This situation is more dire than you've been led to believe. We need to eliminate these creatures and somehow close that gateway. The longer it stays open, the more powerful these things will become."

Malcolm shot him a questioning look.

Hinshaw continued, "Remember the people at the site back in the city? One of those demons is controlling these people.

It's somehow able to influence certain types of people and even gain control over them."

"What types?"

"Evil mannered criminals, more specifically people with a murderous nature." He took a cloth and dropped it over the spilled coffee. "So you see the urgency?"

Malcolm wiped his forehead as he thought of the demons back at the hotel; they were all wearing prison uniforms. "I understand." he said. "I just don't want to risk being caught in another trap. I want to be prepared for anything."

Hinshaw thought for a second. "OK. I'll let you handle a contingency plan. Let me know when you come up with something. You're a good soldier, Malcolm. Let's work together. We've got enough fight on our hands without fighting each other." He stretched out his hand and Malcolm shook it.

"I'll get right on it. Sorry for the—"

"It's OK, I understand." Hinshaw grunted as he knelt down to wipe coffee from the floor.

As Malcolm left the room, he heard Hinshaw shouting for Greg. .

Chapter 16

2:17a.m.

LISA QUIETLY PULLED up a chair and placed it next to Gallois'
bed as Heather slept nearby on a futon. Her eyes were heavy,
but she dreaded the idea of sleeping. Nightmares of her father
came too often.

Leaning forward she took Gallois' hand into hers and
looked at his bruised face. She whispered, "Hey, sleepy head,
it's time to wake up. You're scaring everybody, you know?"

She paused, remembering when they were kids and she had
tried to scare Gallois one early morning. But Gallois had heard
her coming, and she was the one to be freighted. She wished he
would scare her now in the same way. His hand was warm but
completely unresponsive to her touch. It felt like her mother's
hand the day before her death.

She held Gallois hand tighter, pressed it to her cheek and
prayed. Minutes later, she opened her eyes and fought doubts of
her prayers' not having worked for Gallois as they had not for
her mother or father. Letting her head fall on the edge of the
bed, she searched her memories for happier times. But her mind

kept focusing on recent events with her father. She wished she could go back in time and stop them from going. Why didn't she stop them in the first place? She and her father were close. Why didn't she sense what was going to happen to him?

The EEG beeped and startled her.

"Freaking machines," she whispered, resisting the urge to smash the damn thing.

One of her hands was resting on Gallois right wing. She gently rubbed her hand over the lower feathers, finding them to be soft and smooth like a bird's only much larger. She look back at Gallois's matured face wondering how many times he had considered flying away from his glass chamber.

The EEG beeped again and dispensed a readout. More spiking lines.

She noticed Gallois was sweating and went to the bathroom to return with a damp washcloth. She gently dabbed his forehead and was careful not to touch the sensory plugs of the EEG machine. She folded down the bed cover to his waste and was doubly shocked by how fast the wound had healed and how muscular he was. Every one of his muscles was firm and perfectly separated as if they had been sculpted. She laid the washcloth on his abs and slowly began wiping.

She felt the smooth, dense curves of muscles underneath the cloth. She watched his skin react as she slowly worked her way up his chest and to his shoulders. She looked at his abs where water from the cloth had pooled at his belly. She wiped the water and noticed the thin line of hair trailing down into his pants. She wiped the water and, without realizing it, found herself staring at the bulge between his legs underneath the bed sheets. She felt the tips of her fingers moved underneath his pants and jerked her hand away. She looked at Gallois' closed eyes, sure if he were awake, he would be just as confused as she was right now.

What was wrong with her? Sure, as a woman she could not help but notice the changes in his body, but this was Gallois. She could not believe she had allowed herself to think of him that way. She quickly pulled the blanket back up over him. She needed to leave.

She walked out of Gallois' room and down the long hallway. She noticed a soldier standing in a break area.

The soldier smiled at her and said with a thick African accent, "I see I'm not the only one moving about this night."

She returned the smile. "Apparently, I thought I was the only night owl."

"There are many owls in the forest," he said with another smile.

"You have a beautiful accent. Where are you from? I'm guessing Africa"

"You can say that. My name is Khama." He offered his hand, and she took it. Her cell phone chimed. She pulled her phone from her pocket and found Malcolm had sent her a text asking where she was.

"Well, Khama, I'm going to try this sleeping thing again. It was nice to meet you. Don't stay up too late."

"I won't. Good night, Lisa." She was halfway down the hall before she realized she had not told the man her name. When she turned around, he was gone.

Chapter 17

KHAMA WAITED UNTIL Lisa was out of sight before walking to Gallois's room. Entering, he looked down at Heather sleeping uncomfortably on the futon. He waved his hand in her direction, and she let out a sigh as she relaxed. Then he walked over to Gallois' bedside and placed his hand on Gallois's forehead.

"Gallois, second born of the children of Fabian, you have much work to do. But for now, rest and remember nothing."

The EEG machine let out a short series of beeps then printed a read-out of now wavy lines.

"Why did you do that?" Victor asked, standing at the door behind Khama. "We don't need their help."

"Hello, Victor. Still as bitter as ever, I see," Khama said, without turning around.

Victor smirked. "Bidding for the help of humans, I never thought I'd see the day when we'd stoop so low."

Khama turned at last. "As foreseen, the damned are changing the rules, merging the spiritual world with that of man. Soon, they too will have to take up arms in this war."

Victor's brow creased. "This is our war. The charge of dispatching demons was given to us. Not them! Demons must fall by the hands of angels!"

"That is a superficial concern. It matters not by whose hand the enemy falls." Khama walked into the hallway.

"Superficial? Look at the chaos they've caused already. Humans can only worsen the situation. We should leave them to their fate and focus on our duty. Their time draws near anyway. It matters not if it is sooner."

Khama shook his head. "A good servant does as he's told, brother, regardless of his opinion. That's something you forgot and why I now lead."

Victor's eyes shone. "Yes, lead them you did. You led them to be defeated by those mindless beasts."

Khama folded his arms patiently. "That is why I have come. Sean will not willingly exorcise, Mermon and we can not kill humans. Gallois can drive Mermon out of Sean's body. Is your heart so full of resentment that you do not see that?"

"Your confidence in him is unwise. He is but a boy."

"So was David."

Victor eyes narrowed. "We both know this goes farther than Mermon. Interacting with the boy will rouse his curiosity. Have you considered what might happen when he learns the truth about what he is? Nothing corrupts a man's soul like power."

Khama looked at Gallois through the window. "His isolation from the world is an unrealized benefit." Khama nodded. "Yes, one day he will know the truth. When that time comes, I believe his heart will remain pure. You have spent so much time watching him. Why have you not tried to help him?"

"He is not one of us. My concern for him is only for our sake," his voice was cold.

"Why do you dislike him so? Will you never forgive his father?"

Victor's voce was cold. "Because he is not one of us. My concern for him is only for our sake."

"You don't dislike this boy because of anything he has done. You look at him and see his father. When will you finally forgive him?"

Victor scoffed. "Mark my words, Khama. This boy will fail you." He turned his back and disappeared.

Chapter 18

GALLOIS AWOKE FROM the sound of his name being called. He opened his eyes to find Dr. Klein looking down at him. He was groggy as if he were awakening from a week long sleep. He wondered what the doctor had done to make his face hurt so badly.

His mother appeared on the other side of his bed and hugged him, and his whole chest was on fire with pain. "You're not going to be happy until you give me a heart attack, are you?" she said.

His mother released him, and Klein blinded him with the small penlight she pointed into each of his eyes. "How do you feel?"

"Everything hurts." He moved to push himself upright and felt heavy and uncoordinated.

Klein grabbed his arm. "Wait a sec." She pulled the I V out of his hand and removed the sensors from his temples. They looked on as he tried to sit up. The bed responded to the weight of his body as he moved. His wings knocked over several items including the medical dispenser. It was then that he noticed how much larger his wings were.

Heather started to speak but remained silent. She looked to the doctor, who asked, "Gallois, do you remember what happened to you?"

Trying to remember was like looking through a fog. But in the fog, he saw the nightmare that was Sean and remembered the beating he had endured. He looked down at his bare chest and saw the scar left by Mermon's weapon. "He cut me. I couldn't stay in the air." He gasped. "Is Lisa OK?

"She's fine. But I have to tell you something. You were in a coma."

He looked up at her and then his mother. "For how long?"

"Just a few hours, but you developed a mild form of Progeria."

His left eye closed as he looked at her. He did not know what she was talking about, so he ignored her, she did not know how his body worked. And he was not going to help the doctor understand it because he did not trust her. He tried to turn his body to the side of the bed.

Dr. Klein continued, "It's aged you a little, but I don't think it's progressive."

He stopped and looked at her, realizing why they had been looking at him as if they had not seen him in years. He spied the restroom and endured the pain of moving from the bed.

"Easy," his mother warned as she reached under his arm to support the weight of his body.

His mother helped him until he got to the bathroom door. He could not fit his wings through the door until he folded them down. He squeezed through the door and then stared into the mirror. His left eye was black, bruised, and barely open. There were several deep gashes and scrapes on his face that were trying to heal.

He rubbed the stubble on his cheek and stared harder. This was not his face; this face belonged to someone who looked like him, and he was stuck with it. His other hand had rolled into a fist. Blood was coming from his bruised knuckles. He watched blood drip into the sink and run down the drain. He treasured the memory of beating Mermon. But the demon had taken something he could never get back. Hearing the doctor not acknowledge the truth of what had happened to him made it worse. He glared at his image in the mirror.

"Progeria is a childhood disease," he muttered. "A mutation of the lamin A protein in chromosomes. It's nothing like this. He did this to me."

⟶▦◉ ◉▦⟵

Malcolm sat on the side of his bed, tying his boots as Lisa came out of the bathroom. She was wearing her robe and drying her hair with a towel.

"Where are you going?" she asked.

"I have to give Hinshaw something." He finished tying his shoes and then looked around the room.

Lisa pointed to a nearby table. "Your binder is over there on the table."

He noted her tone. "You read it?"

"Yes," she answered casually, turning to go back into the bathroom.

"You shouldn't have done that."

"Shouldn't have read what I'm about to be a part of?"

He lowered his head. She was assuming he had already signed her enlistment forms. He had been so busy with refortifying the building and mission planning that he hadn't found a justification for stalling her enlistment. He took a breath and exhaled.

"I haven't had a chance to turn in your paperwork. Even if I had, no one is going to be worried about processing paperwork right now." It felt like the truth, and it seemed reasonable.

She gave him a long look. He tried not to give away that he had not looked at the forms since she had given them to him.

"But you signed them, right?"

He walked over to the table. He remembered that her enlistment forms were also in the binder.

He turned around. "You already know I didn't." He remembered her father had always been firm with her. He once said he had to be because he had spoiled her and she was used to getting her way. Now that Ramiro was gone, it was up to him. And right now he needed to protect her from herself.

"I'm not going to sign them. You're hurt, angry, and not thinking clearly. That can get you and other people killed. Not to mention the fact that I loved your father too, and allowing you to enlist is exactly what he wouldn't want me to do."

She was looking at him with a stunned expression.

"I'm sorry," he said. "You can hate me if you want. But I'm going to keep you safe because it's what he would've wanted and I love you."

It seemed like hours before her stare softened. She walked over and hugged him. Her head rested on his shoulder. The robe was damp, and she smelled of sweet shampoo.

"I love you too. I am sorry for asking you to do that. I know you want to protect me. But that's not what I want." She released him. "I want to fight, and I don't need your permission. I not mad at you for not helping me. I hope you won't be mad at me for doing what I needed to do."

He looked into her guilty eyes. "What did you do?"

"I enlisted with Hinshaw's men."

"You went behind my back?"

She shook her head. "Don't make it like that. You knew I wanted this, just like I knew you would fight me on it. What did you expect me to do?"

"I expected you to wait. Now you've—" He shook his head. He was about to say that she had made it so he could not watch over her, which is exactly what she did not want. He snatched the folder from the table.

"Malcolm, it's my choice. "You should be supportive of that."

"You would say that because it's always about what you want. Did you even think about how this was going to affect our relationship? What do you think happens when this is over, assuming we survive? You're one of his soldiers. When this is over, you'll have to go with him."

He read her facial expression and could not determine if she hadn't considered the consequences. Maybe she was willing to end their relationship. Both outcomes seemed like the same.

"I expect you trust me! Now you've—" He shook his head. He was about to say that she had made it so he couldn't watch over her which is exactly what she didn't want. He snatched the folder from the table.

"Malcolm it's my choice. You should be supportive of that."

"Yeah, you would say that. As usual you just thought about what you wanted and not about how it was going to affect us! That's even if you considered me at all. You do realize it don't you? You're part of his unit. When this is over you'll have to go with him."

He read her facial expression and could not determine if she hadn't considered the consequences. Maybe she was willing to end their relationship. Both possibilities made him feel as though his love for her was something she would disregard.

He did not want to hear the answer. Her cell phone chimed, and she actually checked it. He stormed out of the room, leaving her with something that was more important than their relationship.

--->===◉ ◉===<---

Gallois was sitting on a rolling stool eating a large meal when Lisa rushed into his room. His wings were spread, and he was only wearing some now tighter hospital pajamas. Muscle surrounded the area around his wings. His biceps and pectoral muscles flexed as he ate.

"How are you, big guy?" she said cheerfully. "You had us scared there for a moment."

"Sorry," his said in a deeper but still very "Gallois" voice.

"Where's your mother?"

"She's changing clothes."

"How do you feel? I mean, other than hungry?"

"Fine, I guess." His expression saddened. "The doctor said I've aged about five years."

"Hey! That means we're the same age," She said brightly.

He looked down at his plate. "I lost five years of my life."

She placed her hand on his shoulder. "You've got many more years left." She looked at his pants, which had been crudely cut to accommodate his wings and size. "But those clothes won't make it much longer."

"Yeah," Gallois said with a chuckle.

Chapter 19

MALCOLM SALUTED AND placed the folder on Hinshaw's desk.

"Is this it?" Hinshaw asked opening the folder.

"Yes. I'm confident that, if needed, we'll be prepared."

"Good," Hinshaw's eyes roamed over the documents. "Good idea using the building down the street. The garage should be big enough to hold a lot of soldiers and maybe a tank."

Malcolm paused, waiting for the right moment to ask him the question tugging on his mind. "Sir, I have a problem that I was hoping you could help me with."

Hinshaw lowered the folder. "Concerning?"

"Lisa Vasquez. She's just enlisted with your unit."

"Yes, I remember her. She came and asked me directly. She seems like a real go getter. Here I am expecting soldiers to come asking to be released." He laid the binder on the desk. "I had the Vatican e-mail her file. She's the daughter of your lieutenant, right? He did a great job training her. I think she's going to be a great soldier."

"Well, he let her go through the training, but he never intended for her to go into active duty. It's possible her father has been killed by the Nesphar. Her motive for joining is for confrontation."

"I'm sure it is. Under the circumstances, that's what I need. A soldier who's not afraid of these things."

"I understand. I just don't think her father would have approved. Actually, I know it."

Hinshaw leaned back in his chair, eyes narrowed. "I see. You want me to give her the boot for her father? The problem is, I've already accepted her. And even if I hadn't, I don't think that would stop her." He leaned further back in the chair and folded his arms. "I understand how you feel. This is what I will do: I'll make sure she stays out of reach of these things."

Malcolm nodded. "OK. Thank you, sir."

Hinshaw stood up and walked over to an aerial photograph of the city. "We're going to hit the building tomorrow at sunset."

He joined Hinshaw in front of the aerial photograph.

Hinshaw's fat index finger pointed to buildings circled in red. "My men have set up surveillance cameras around the buildings adjacent to this location. We've gained some valuable intel. The demons' influence must be getting stronger. Numerous people have been flocking to the building since we discovered it. We've identified most of them as members of the Nesphar. The rest are unarmed civilians. We're assuming they are possessed because they just walk around all day without resting or eating. It won't take long once we're inside to be sure."

He pointed to a blurry picture with various red marks on it. "Right now infrared scanners show at least 300 people on the upper levels. We're not sure how many below. There's no way of determining how far down the lower levels are but our scientists say the surrounding geological information suggests it can only go down about a mile, maybe a mile and a half." He took a deep breath. "It's going to be gruesome."

"What about the larger lead demons? Any sign of where they are?"

"We only were able to locate two of the four demons. Here's one at the top of the building. I guess he's a lookout. He's accompanied by only a few freaks. The other is here at the building's center. The last two are most likely guarding the gateway." Hinshaw took off his hat and wiped his balding head. "They stay hidden until sunset. We'll attack then. I don't want to deal with those things all at once. We improve our chances by separating their numbers."

Malcolm nodded in agreement, and Hinshaw continued, "A large number of my men will enter the facility and split off into two groups. Your group, will make its way to the lower level. Your objective will be to kill the last two demons. I'm sure one of them is in charge of the others. Hopefully, without him the number of possessed people will drop. He shouldn't be too hard to find. The other group will move to the middle level, where a team from the roof will meet with them."

"What about the demon on the roof?"

"An armed helicopter will be waiting. That demon will be cut to pieces before the helicopter lands. Then they'll make their way downstairs, where we should already be in contact with the last of them. Together, they should have enough of an arsenal to deal with the rest of the possessed people you encounter below.

Upon your exit, you will set C4 charges around that gateway, detonate it on your way out, and close it for good."

Malcolm tapped on the file in his hand. "Any group needs help, a team will be waiting to assist."

"And if we fail, I've authorized a strike force to level that place and everything in it. The Vatican says it won't solve the overall problem, but it will give them time to develop another plan."

"What about our men inside?" Malcolm asked.

"They'll have fifteen minutes to get out. These creatures' numbers have been increasing. It could take weeks for the Vatican to convince the government to take more drastic measures. The Vatican only has a small amount of influence with them. The government's belief in the supernatural goes only so far." He put his hat back on, "it's just been a few days, and those demons already have hundreds in support. I'd hate to see how many they will have in another week "

"Do you need me to do anything else, general?"

"No, just make sure your men are ready. I've been preparing mine for this since we returned"

"OK." Malcolm saluted.

Hinshaw did the same. "Make sure they're well rested. And get some rest yourself. It's going to be a long day."

Chapter 20

MALCOLM ENTERED THE restroom across from the room
Hinshaw was using as an office. Two Knights were exiting and
they exchanged greetings. He walked over to the sink, turned
on the faucet, and listened for the door to close. Then he rushed
into one of the stalls knelt over the toilet, and vomited. He
stayed there with his head held over the toilet until the nausea
passed.

Then he flushed and returned to the sink to rinse his
mouth. He spat into the basin and stood there with his head
held low. Images of the demons flashed through his head and
drowned all optimism. He kept telling himself that the demons
could not take his soul to hell. He wanted to believe what he
had been raised to believe. He wanted to believe that God decided who went to hell.

But no matter how hard he tried, he could not convince
himself that he was worthy of heaven, so he thought of the
only positive outcome of his conversation with Hinshaw. He
hoped the man would be true to his word and keep Lisa off
the frontlines of battle, but Hinshaw had shown that he did

not care about a teenage boy. It was hard to believe that he would he care about her. He understood all too well the mind of a soldier. If it came down to it, Hinshaw would use her. She was tool to be used for the completion of the mission. They all were.

~>→=® ®=→<~

He thought about the argument he and Lisa had earlier. He did not want to be angry with her. Today might be their last day together, the last day he had to show her how much he loved her, the last day to make her understand. With that thought, he resigned himself to the idea of apologizing to her. He left the restroom and made his way to their room.

~>→=® ®=→<~

Malcolm opened the door to his room and called for his love. Lisa was not there. The only other place she would be was in Gallois' room. He turned around and walked down the hall that led to the infirmary and again realized that he had not thought much about Gallois. Although he never particularly liked him, he felt bad for not checking on the boy. The young man had shown more courage than he could ever have expected. Not only had he risked his life to stop the Nesphar, he had saved Lisa's life.

He saw Dr. Klein coming out of her office and called to her.

"Oh, hi, Malcolm," Klein returned. She seemed more relaxed than the last time he had seen her.

"How's Gallois doing?"

She gave him an awkward glance. "He's fine. He woke not too long ago and has been troublesome ever since." She smiled. "But I'm glad he's wake. You should go see him." She walked into a room across the hall.

Before he could make a move he heard Lisa laughing. He had not heard that sound in days. As he walked further down the hall, Lisa's laughter got louder. He looked in through the glass window, and his eyes widened.

Gallois was not a lanky teenager any more, but a full-grown man. Heather was looking on as he held Lisa above his head with one hand pressed against her stomach. Gallois' arms were huge. He did not seem to have any trouble holding her aloft. His lover smiled the way she had when they first met. He loved her smile; it reached down into his soul and made him feel special, like he was the only man in the world that could make her that happy.

Gallois grabbed her waist as he lowered her to the floor. They were chest to chest. She smiled at him and looked at his lips before turning away. There was something in her eyes; Malcolm had seen it before on the night of their seconded date. They had been standing the same distance apart, and he wondered if he should kiss her. The look in her eyes told him that he should.

Heather saw him looking in on them. "Malcolm! Come here," she called.

He walked into the room and forced a smile as he looked at Gallois. "Hi. I see you're awake. How do you feel?"

"I'm OK."

"What are you guys doing in here? The doctor said you've been causing trouble."

"We were just having a little fun with her," Heather said. "She's been running in and out of here checking and double-checking on Gallois. I told her that she was too old for my son." She and Lisa laughed.

Malcolm looked at Lisa. "Yeah, he's only fifteen."

Lisa pointed to Gallois' arms. "Well, he doesn't look it! Look at these arms, Malcolm."

Malcolm wanted to punch him. "He's gotten big. What did the doctor give him?"

"The doctor said it was a form of progeria, but he's fine now," Lisa said.

Heather moved some things from the futon. "Sit down, Malcolm, and stay awhile."

"Sorry. I can't. I just came to tell Lisa something. Well, I guess I might as well tell all of you. We believe we have found Sean. We're going after him tomorrow."

"What about the demons?" Gallois asked.

"They are there with him. We are going to eliminate all of them."

"Sweet Jesus," Heather whispered.

Malcolm gave Lisa a scolding look. "Since Lisa has become a member, she needs to get some rest tonight as well."

Heather turned to Lisa with a stunned expression. "Lisa you didn't enlist did you?"

She fidgeted. Her eyes roamed from Heather to Gallois. "I was waiting for the right time to tell you two."

Gallois had a worried expression on his bruised face.

"Why did you do that? Your father didn't want you to be a Knight," Heather said.

"My father is dead," she snapped before looking at Malcolm with a reddened face. "I'm sorry, Ms. Henning, I didn't mean to—I have to do this. I'm sorry." She started walking to the exit. Heather grabbed her and hugged her tightly.

"I better get some rest," Lisa said. I'll see you two tomorrow." Malcolm reached for her hand as she walked out of the room, and she ignored it. He said goodnight to Gallois and his mother before following her out of the room.

⟶▪▭◉ ◉▭▪⟵

Malcolm closed the door to his room, turned around, and saw Lisa's eyes on him.

"Why did you do that?" she asked. "I was going to tell them. I didn't need your help."

"Does it matter? It needed to be said. Or were you going to tell them tomorrow as you were leaving?"

She stared at him a moment and then rolled her eyes before sitting down on the bed. She dropped her head into her open palms and took a breath. "What time do we leave tomorrow?"

"In the evening."

"Is he sure it's the right place?"

"Positive."

She pulled back her hair. "So it's really going to happen tomorrow?"

"Isn't that what you wanted?"

She did not answer him. She dropped her head and stared at the floor. Then she clasped her hands together, but he could still see they were shaking.

He walked over and knelt down in front of her. "Don't be afraid," he said, placing his hands on top of hers.

Her voice was almost a whisper. "I don't think I can do it."

"You can, and you will. You already know how to do it. You've trained with us long enough. All you have to do is pull the trigger."

He rubbed her back. "It's OK to be afraid. But don't let that stop you. That's the difference. Remember what your father taught you."

She wrapped her arms around him. "I love you," she said in a shaky voice. She took off his hat and let it fall to the floor and then ran her fingers through his hair. His hand moved to the bottom of her shirt then up underneath it. He kissed her hard as he caressed her breast. She lifted his shirt off and leaned back on the bed. "I love you too."

Chapter 21

GALLOIS LAY ON his hospital bed staring at the television as he thought of how he could ask Hinshaw not to allow Lisa to fight with them tomorrow. But each of his ideas fell flat under the weight of the mission's importance. This left him with the last-resort idea of just showing up tomorrow in uniform; surely the general would not deny his involvement after what he had done to help. But forcing the general's hand did not seem wise even though there were two things he was dead-set on: Lisa was not going in there without him, and, if Mermon showed up, he was flying her out of there.

He had no intention of staying in the hospital despite his mother's insistence. She was using his injuries as an excuse to keep him bedridden. From the corner of his eye, he watched as she sat on the futon. Like the calm before the storm, it had been an hour since Lisa and Malcolm had left the room, and neither of them had said more than ten words, which made him grateful for the television.

Unfortunately, the silence was to both of their advantages. He had no doubt that his mother was prepared to rebut anything he suggested that could serve as a reason for getting involved in the mission. Without warning, his mother cut her eyes in his direction, something she usually did when she knew he was watching her. He realized that he had intentionally given her the "go signal," and with all his pondering, he had not prepared for a battle of words. He turned his head back to the television. Feeling like a cornered animal, he waited.

She spoke in a firm tone. "You've done all you can do. There's nothing else to be done."

"I can go in with them tomorrow," he said, looking grave.

"Gallois, there'll be shooting. Let them handle it. It's what they've trained for. You'd only get in the way."

"Not if I ask them tomorro—"

"I said no, now!" she snapped, "You've done enough! I know I told you that I wouldn't stop you. But I'm not going to let you kill yourself. Look what happened to you last time. The doctor didn't know what was wrong with you. You could've died!" She took a breath, walked over and gently took his face in her hands. "Listen. I understand what you're going through. I know you're angry and hurt. I am too. I cared about Ramiro and Father Jacob just as much as you do. You think I don't feel like grabbing a gun too?"

Gallois turned away partly because hearing the words was like picking at a wound but mostly because he believed she had purposely left his father's name cut. He was the first person who had been cursed by his birth. She would never admit it but there was a time when even she resented him. He remembered the first years at the church, the long spans of time between visits, the half-hugs and the look in her eyes when she would say she loved him. To gain her love and forgiveness, he had always tried to be the good son. But he could not do that anymore, and the words left his month with more firmness than he had intended: "I'm not going to hide anymore."

His mother's eyes widened and then narrowed. "I didn't know that I had raised such a selfish child. When did this become just about you?" She leaned closer. "Because that's the only opinion you seemed interested in, even though we've both had to live through all of this. What about me? Have you given any thought as to how your decisions affect me? Do you have any idea what I've been going through these last few days?"

She placed a hand on his forearm. "I am your mother. I have loved you since the day you were born. You have no idea what it's like for a parent to watch their child risk his life at every opportunity. Well, let me help you understand. It's a nightmare. I can't sleep. I can't eat from worrying about you. Can't you see? If you keep doing this, it's going to get you killed. And I could not handle that. The child is supposed to bury the parent not the other way around." She put her hand on his arm. "I've never asked you for anything." She squeezed. "I'm asking now. Stop this. I'm begging you. Please stop."

Gallois was conflicted by his love for his mother and for Lisa. He could not tell her that he had already weighted the pros and cons of his not being around and determined she would be better off. Yet seeing her like this almost balanced the scale. His only possible comeback was that he loved her enough to die for her happiness. But it had to go unsaid. Nonetheless, he used his reserve to hold fast and remain silent even though his love for her begged for him to give in. After a few seconds that felt like hours, his mother's face shifted into a sad expression that stung his tear ducts. Then she left the room.

Feeling like the worst son in the world, Gallois let his head drop back on his pillow. He stared at the ceiling for several minutes reflecting on his mother's expression. Was he being selfish? He took a moment and tried to see things from her position, but the benefits of his not being around made it very difficult. Contemplation rendered doubt as he slid down on the bed rubbing his temples.

He felt overwhelmed, but he knew in his heart he was doing the right thing. Protecting those you love couldn't be wrong even if it caused them grief. Hopefully his mother would come to understand afterwards. He had to do this.

The starry night caught his attention as he reached for a cup of orange juice resting on the nightstand. Open sky was just what he needed. He yearned to feel nothing but air moving around him, nothing below or around, to be totally free of the world, to forget about everything including himself.

The night air was warm as Gallois stretched his wings on the roof. Drawing a deep breath he looked up at the stars and stepped onto the ledge. Forewarning iced down his back. Someone is there. He spun around angrily, expecting to find Victor's cold gaze on him. "Stay away from me!" he yelled, not caring if rudeness got him thrown into another wall.

At that moment he felt a calming aura come over him as a bright white light shone before him. The combination of the two sent him to his knees covering his eyes. As the light began to dim, he returned his gaze to find large black wings appearing from the light. When the light diminished, a male angel was standing before him.

Gallois's eyes slowly trailed up to the angel's athletic frame and handsome face. The angel wore black sandals and a Chiton similar to Victor's, but it was dark brown, two shades darker than the angel's skin tone. Hanging from his waist was a glimmering gold sword and scabbard both secured by a black sword belt.

The angel smiled with high cheek bones and full lips. "You must have been visited by Victor. Your anger is understandable. Victor has a way of irritating people." He reached out his hand. "Please stand, Gallois."

Awestruck, Gallois took the angel's hand but was afraid to look the divine being in the face as he stood.

"My name is Khama. I lead the Guardian Angels in this part of your world. I'm sorry for Victor's rudeness. He is one of the few angels who distain humans."

Relief overtook Gallois as he took the meaning of this encounter as an end to all their troubles; relief and amazement knotted in his throat. He had to force his tongue loose. "You're a Guardian Angel? My mother told me about you. She said you protect us from demons. Is he, is Victor one of you?" Gallois hoped not. If Victor were, he was more than ready to report him for abandoning his duty the night his father had been taken.

"Your mother was right. And no, Victor isn't one of us. He is what we call a Drifter. Angels are sent to earth with a job; some are sent to fight, some to heal and some to influence. But Drifters are angels who have abandoned their duty or lost the privilege to do it."

"How do they lose their job?"

Khama smiled. "Angels have free will just like humans. Some angels choose to end their service; others are deemed unworthy by the Father and stripped of their duty and all powers bestowed for that duty. Although both experiences are traumatic for angels the latter is the worst because it means that angel has fallen out of favor with the Father. Most often when this happens the angel blames humans for his misfortune and resents them."

"What was Victor's job before he became a Drifter?"

"He was a Guardian Angel." Khama placed a hand on Gallois' shoulder. "Now I have a question for you. Why do you think an angel's duty is so important to him?"

Feeling put on the spot, Gallois thought for several seconds before taking a jab at an answer from one of Father Jacob's sermons: "Because servitude is the highest form of praise."

Khama smiled again and nodded. "That's correct Gallois, and that is why I have come to you this night. I am here to ask you to help me serve the Father."

Gallois' heart skipped a beat. What help could he possibility offer an angel? He tried to speak, but nothing came out.

Khama gave a compassionate gaze. "I know it seems as though we have been blind to your troubles with the Nesphar, but we have not. We have not intervened because there are rules that must be followed."

"Rules?"

"Yes. There are two rules that both Angels and Demons must obey; the first is easier for humans to understand than the second, and that is that we cannot take a human life. We can only influence you in this trial that you call life. The second rule is that no angel or demon can walk this earth in their true form. You see, in our natural realm of existence, we have no need for a physical body, and as the historical leaders of your world have proven, the spirit is far more powerful than the body."

Gallois frowned. He could accept the idea these hideous creatures were not full-fledged demons far easier than the notion that the people he'd loved were not killed by demons. "But they're still breaking the rules, aren't they? People are dying because of them."

"You must understand, Mermon and his demons are like conduits. They are powerless without man's will empowering them. Only once have they broken a rule. Unfortunately, upon doing so they've been able to persuade more to serve them."

"So why don't you break the rule too? I mean, if it would stop them."

Khama shook his head. "Angels don't break the rules."

Shame shot through Gallois as he realized how his suggestion must have sounded. But he'd grown desperate to save what little remained of his life. "So you won't help us fight them?"

"We will always help you, for it is the will of the Father. He has not given up on you. That is why I have come, to tell you of a plan I have to send Mermon and his minions back into darkness."

Khama eyes trailed to Gallois' wings. "It is written, the Father has plans for all of us. Therefore we are created as we are for a purpose. The faithful and wise take comfort in that."

Gallois' head lowered with shame and disappointment as the page Jeremiah 21:11 flashed in his photographic memory like the reemergence of a wronged friend. He'd found comfort in the passage for nearly two years before depression had tarnished its value. Even now hearing it referenced by this celestial being did little to tilt the scale. Gallois' eyes were stinging. He did his best not to show his sadness, but this second end-all answer hurt worse than even with Victor.

"Gallois, I have come to ask you to take part in my plan, but doing so will require you to accept who you are."

Gallois's brows arched. What help could he possibly offer an angel?

"Gallois, the weapons the demons are using make it difficult for us to get to Mermon. You've seen them right, that night in the alley?"

"Yes, it made me feel weak. Victor said that it was my father's blood. Was he telling the truth?"

"I am sorry, but yes."

Even greater fear took hold of Gallois at the thought of having been beaten with his father's blood. Since he was the product of his father, it felt like Mermon had already killed him once.

"Your father was once an angel. When he chose to live as a human, he became a Descender. The blood of a Descender can be fatal to angels and, as you witnessed, others with angelic ancestry."

"You want me to help you get the weapons?"

"No. The weapons are only an inconvenience. The main concern lies with Mermon. He is one of the Fallen, one of the original Lost Souls casted out of heaven with Satan. That means he is a lead demon and has the power to summon other demons at will. His presence here in your world means Sean has found the Pit of Lost Souls, the place where the Fallen landed on earth after their banishment. The Pit acts as a gateway where demons wait to be released on earth. With each passing day since Mermon came here, the number of demons in your world has doubled. As I've said, the rules forbid us from harming humans. With his numbers now, we cannot get to Mermon without breaking that rule. I want you to face Sean and lure Mermon out of his body. Mermon is the source of this turmoil, not Sean."

New fear smacked Gallois in the face. He turned, hoping his facial expression hadn't given that away. The thought of standing in front of that impossible creature again made him tremble. Dying wasn't as quick and easy as he'd thought it would be. Mermon wouldn't let it be easy.

He closed his eyes and held his breath as childhood nightmares of his father's suffering at the hands of demons fast-forwarded in his head. He thought of how true those nightmares must have been for his father. It was his turn now to risk his life for others, and he was ashamed at how much he didn't feel up to the challenge. He exhaled and thought if he could just get the words out, could let the answer in his heart be a leap of faith. "Okay. I'll try to draw him out. But there are so many of them."

"Be of good faith. We will be with you. You won't see us, but we will be there."

Gallois tilted his head. "I'll have to ask the general first. He's probably not going to be OK with my going again."

"I'll take care of that. Tomorrow when you speak to him, he will want you to be a part of the mission."

Gallois paused, thinking of his mother. "If something happens. . ."

"Fear not. The Shepherd is always watching over his flock. Your mother will be taken care of." Khama turned to the door leading from the roof and turned his head over his shoulder. "When it's time, I will have some clothes for you that should prove useful." Gallois nodded, and in a blink Khama disappeared.

Chapter 22

HINSHAW STOOD ON a podium in the underground hanger of the site. Malcolm stood just behind him with a few other officers. He glanced down at Lisa standing in uniform in the crowd. They exchanged looks. The room was packed with soldiers holding guns of varying types. Military vehicles and two tanks encircled the soldiers and were parked facing the open hanger door that let in the heat of the afternoon sun. There was an atmosphere of fear and anticipation. Every soldier's eyes were fixed on Hinshaw as he stood observing the room.

"Soldiers, you already have been briefed on this mission. The time has come to execute!" He walked away from the podium. "Now, I'm supposed to give you an uplifting speech. I'm supposed to say something to ensure your determination and boast your morale. Truth is, I can't think of anything that would be more apparent than what you have already witnessed. You know what you're fighting for! You're fighting for America's core beliefs: freedom, independence, and the right to pursue happiness! You're fighting for your immediate family and all, whether he is on our shores or not! Weather he wants it or not!

Why?" He leaned forward. "Because throughout man's history these are the most prevalent necessities of life! Without them life becomes less than unlivable, less than what we believe the good Lord intended for us! Fortunately he gives us the means to prevent this!"

He took a gun from Malcolm and set it out before the soldiers. "I admit a few are ugly and incomprehensible, like many other things about life. It's better for us not to try to understand why God does what he does because his wisdom far exceeds ours. We should just trust him and do the best we can in this life. Having said that, I'd like to commend you on the ass whipping you put on those demons back in the city!"

The bay room erupted in cheers. Soldiers pumped their guns in the air while gesturing to each other. "But our work's not done yet! We've got them on the run! Like roaches, they've buried themselves behind the walls of this building and infested it with more of their kind! It's time to finish the extermination process!"

The soldiers shouted again, some clanging their weapons against vehicles, their faces rigid with determination. Hinshaw gripped the gun and smiled and raised the gun in the air. "Let's go give it to them! Happy hunting, soldiers! Hooh-rah!"

The soldiers yelled, "Hooh-rah!" in unison as they sprinted to their vehicles. Malcolm and Lisa locked eyes before she moved with the rest of the men. They mouthed, "I love you," before she hurried with the others.

"Is he ready?" Malcolm asked Hinshaw as they walked from the podium.

"Yes. I spoke to Gallois before this meeting. Once we have set up a resistance he will join us and enter the building. We need to give him as much support as possible without compromising our objective. He seems sure that his plan will work. I believe him. Just concentrate on getting to that lower level."

"Yes, sir, we'll be ready for him."

Gallois pulled up the pants of the outfit Khama had left in his room. The pants and shoes were dark tan and included a light tan sleeveless shirt. The whole outfit had similar embroidery along its sides like his old clothes with slits to allow his wings to extend.

He pulled the shirt over his head and looked in a mirror. Everything fit perfectly. He felt the material of the shirt. He'd never felt anything like it before. He looked back in the mirror and slowly extended his wings, surprised at how well the outfit's color and trim complemented his body. But like every other good thought he'd had today, the opinion was soon overshadowed by the possibility of today's being the day of his death. His only comfort for his fear was the five-page letter he'd written and stashed with his things for his mother to find.

His mother appeared at the door and stopped and looked him over in astonishment. Slowly her hands rose to her chest before overlapping each other. "Your father, he was wearing that when I first saw him." She went over to him and felt his shirt. "Where did you get this?"

"An angel named Khama left it for me."

"Khama? Your father spoke of him, but I've never seen him."

She paused. "You'll be leaving soon?"

Gallois nodded.

"Baby, I'm sorry about last night. I understand why you're doing this."

"You don't have to apologize, Mom."

Tears were in her eyes. "You're right for doing this, for fighting back." She forced a laugh. "Sometimes the child teaches the parent."

A communicator lying next to the pair of gloves that went with the outfit sounded. Gallois picked it up and put it to his ear. "Yes. OK, I'm coming." He fastened a tracking device to the underside of his shirt and picked up his gloves.

"Time to go?" Heather asked.

"Yes. Will you come with me to the roof?"

Gallois opened the door to the roof, and they walked out to the ledge at a pace regulated by his mother's short steps and halting grip around his arm. She exhaled slowly. Her gaze was on the horizon, but her thoughts weren't. Her hold on his hand and arm tightened and he could feel her shaking.

She turned to him smiling with her lips but not her eyes, "You be careful. Come back to me."

"I will," he said, trying to sound as reassuring as possible. He placed his free hand on her arm, matching the pressure of her grip before gently pulling away from her. As he stepped onto the concrete rail he exposed his wings through the narrow slits in his shirt. "I love you, Mom," he said quickly, and sincerely before flying off.

When he was a quarter mile away, he looked back at his mother's small figure with the sinking feeling that he'd never see her again.

Chapter 23

"WE HAVE A hostile situation! I repeat! The civilians are hostile. Over!" shouted a soldier from Hinshaw's radio.

Hinshaw was in his mobile command post at the end of a caravan of intercepting soldiers and vehicles outside Sean's building. Hinshaw grabbed his radio from the dashboard. "Copy that, soldier. All men, fire at will! I repeat, fire at will! Operation Fireman is in motion! Team Two, be advised, we are opening the door at the east end."

"Copy, sir. Team two is ready to proceed," Malcolm reported.

Hinshaw gripped the radio firmly. "Tank Two, open up that bee hive!"

With two loud cannon blasts, pieces of the front of Sean's building exploded into a cloud of debris.

"Get ready to move!" Malcolm shouted to a large group of soldiers squatting with him.

After the dust from the blasts settled, they moved in sequence up to the side of the hole. A large helicopter arrived on the scene and vanished over the top of the building as Malcolm peered into the opening. Pieces of civilian bodies were lying scattered around the hole. He could see the other team of soldiers in the distance shooting at possessed people.

There were more possessed people than he and Hinshaw had expected. They were fighting like rabid animals, the same as before, undeterred by the soldiers' weapons against their unarmed freakish physicality. When one creature fell, others advanced in its place. They would soon overwhelm the soldiers.

"Move!" Malcolm barked, and he and his men entered the site, guns blasting. Some of the creatures turned their attention to them. More soldiers followed them and joined in firing. Malcolm gestured, and along with a few men he split off and headed toward a door leading to the basement.

Lisa crouched down along the side of the helicopter door as a soldier fired a six-barrel M134 Minigun. The bullets sent scattered pieces of concrete and specks of blood flying as it tore through the bodies of possessed men bustling onto the roof in a wave of ferocity. "Do you see it?" he called to Lisa. It was getting dark. The helicopter lights shone on the roof, but it was still hard to see in the overcast.

"No. Still no visual on the Demon!"

"Forget it then! Just take out everything! We're going to have to go—wait, there it is! The lead demon is on your nine! See him?"

"Got it!" The soldier fired, but the creature dodged the rounds. "Get us lower!" he yelled to the pilot. The chopper descended, and the gunner kept trying to hit the Demon while killing possessed men. But he couldn't get a bead on it as the creature dodged repeatedly, sometimes using one of the possessed as a shield.

As Lisa continued firing along with him, her ears rang from the sounds of the gun and bullet shells hitting the floor. Suddenly she realized that they were closer than expected to the rooftop. "You're too low! Get up!" She looked back at the Demon. Too late. It jumped onto the helicopter's windshield and was making its way for the pilot. Lisa held onto a latch and stuck her arm out and around the helicopter door. She fired, hitting the Demon a few times in the leg before it had a chance to move.

"C'mon, kill it!" the pilot screamed hopelessly.

Lisa watched but couldn't get a clear shot. If she shot the glass the shards could seriously injure the pilot. She had to wait until it broke through. But that would be too late. At that point some possessed men jumped onto the helicopter's landing gear. The other soldiers fired on them. Still more possessed men climbed onto the dangling men, using their bodies to form a ladder. The helicopter bobbed and weaved as the pilot began to lose control.

Lisa lost her balance and fell to the floor. A soldier was yelling something into his radio. She couldn't make out what he was saying, but she heard Hinshaw's bolstering voice. They weaved again, more violently than before. They were going to crash.

⇥⚙ ⚙⇤

Gallois darted in between the city buildings, wings flapping rhythmically and arms at his sides. It was late enough that night was nearly falling, and he'd go unnoticed unless he flew too low. He stayed so high that, if someone were to look, up they would think he was some sort of large bird like a hawk. Tilting his left wing, he darted left and soon saw what General Hinshaw said he would see: numerous rows of red and blue police lights flashing as they blocked all road entrances to Sean's building for two miles. He flew past the road blocks, and after a mile he could see the military vehicles and Sean's building in the clearing ahead. Static sounded over his communicator, and Hinshaw's voice boomed, "OK, Gallois. It's ready. Look for my man!"

"Copy!" Gallois said, tucking his wings into a dive as he reached the clearing before leveling out into a glide above advancing squads of soldiers scrabbling from transport vehicles. No sooner than when he had passed the last squad, he heard the cacophony of automatic gun fire, howls, and screams, most coming from the large hole in the building just 300 yards ahead. Gathering his courage, he continued on and soon spotted a lone soldier ahead of him standing atop a van. The soldier was raising two grenade belts high over his head. Gallois grabbed them as he flew by and neared the hole in Sean's building.

Inside the hole he could see the soldiers fighting off the possessed people. More soldiers were entering the site as they battled. He saw Lisa's helicopter bobbing in the air with the Demons and possessed clinging to it and soared upward. The creatures had punched a hole in the window and grabbed the pilot by the shirt. The helicopter was starting to tilt on its side. With one powerful thrust Gallois shot forward. He grabbed the Demon by its foot and carried it high in the air. The Demon hissed and growled as it tried to free itself.

Gallois flew above the roof and dropped the Demon before pulling pins of from the grenade belt. The pins and grenades were falling below the Demon. Gallois hovered and watched the horrible explosion of body parts. The remains of the beast splattered onto the concrete roof.

Gallois pulled his wings close to his body and entered a dive. His speed increased as he descended. Lisa and the other soldiers had killed the possessed hanging from the landing gear and were preparing to land on the roof where only a few possessed people remained.

"I'm going inside," Gallois reported.

Hinshaw acknowledged the assertion, and then Gallois heard the voice of another man with an African accent reporting that his team had cleared the first level and was now moving to the second. Gallois inverted and flew into the building through the tank, blasted opening. He felt like he was flying over a mass grave. The smelled of sulfur and gunpowder. He tried not to look at the mutilated bodies, but it was impossible to ignore so much death. He saw two soldiers motioning to him as they held open double doors; they were covered in dirt and blood, and he could not determine if the blood were theirs. He flew through the doors and entered a crudely built corridor made of drywall and plywood flooring tracked with dirt and dried mud. Endless string construction lights hung loosely down the center of the ceiling and flickered in sync with the whirling noises coming from small machines positioned yards apart.

There was static when Hinshaw's voice sounded over the communicator. "Gallois you're descending underground. We're going to lose radio contact. Expect trouble once you meet up with Malcolm's team." The connection was already breaking up.

"Roger that," Gallois said as he felt fear rising up within him. He could not give into it; too many people were depending on him. Khama was depending on him. He could not fail them. He kept his eyes on the darkness ahead. There was nothing in his path except what appeared to be small medical machines. When he reached the darkness, his surroundings abruptly changed, as if those who had built the corridor had runout of plaster and string lights. He was now surrounded by rugged earth, and dropped flares lit the way forward. The flares hissed as they burned, reminding him of the only reptile that he wished did not exist. Light danced on the earth walls and played evil tricks on his eyes.

Like a bat, he swayed lift, right then right again down the corridor. Nothing obstructed his path. There wasn't anything in the corridor but a few gurneys and medical equipment and endless unpolished floor and darkness ahead. After another few yards, the smell of sulfur, mud and decay began to fill his nostrils; intensifying the further he flew like a repellent against sanity. Still Gallois flew on through the now winding path, increasing his speed with each thrust of his wings, growing increasingly worried that he'd arrive too late to help Malcolm and the soldiers. Gallois banked a hard right as the path suddenly shifted and found an end of the concrete walls and lights, leaving in their place a cave of earth, loose dirt and burning flares that were no doubt left by Malcolm's men. The darkness was getting thicker. The construction stopped, and he found himself in a cave. Earth surrounded him.

There were footprints near the flares. He recognized them as those of the army issue boots he had seen most of his life. His telepathy sent its eerie warning seconds before he heard the distant sounds of gunfire, growls, and human screams. The sounds grew louder as he approached an opening with streaks of light and demonic shadows dashing about. He flew into the opening and collided with a demon. He fell on top of it, and their bodies took two other demons down with them.

When he saw the demon's face, it was already biting down into his shoulder. He felt the pain in his neck, but it was nothing compared to the jolting agony of the next bite into his thigh. That was the only reason he was able to get to his feet with so much speed that it freed him from the jaws of both demons.

As he kicked both demons in the face, other demons jumped on his back and clung onto his wings. The muscles in his back were his strongest, and he was able to toss the demons off and return to the air. He circled the cavern and watched as dozens of possessed men and women of various shapes and sizes roared as they trampled over the corpses of their fallen comrades in a effort to traverse a barrage of bullets fired by Malcolm and his team, who were pinned down on the other side of the cavern.

Bullets from the soldiers' weapons shredded the creatures' clothes and mangled their bodies in ways that would have killed anything human, but few demons fell in comparison to the number of bullets fired. Moreover for each demon that fell another seemed to appear. Gallois saw why the demons' numbers weren't diminishing. They were entering the cavern from a break in the wall next to a concrete support beam.

Between the break and the soldiers was a gaping sixteen-foot pit, the reason so many had died, barely visible in the darkness. At first, he mistook the white matter rising at the edge of the pit for smoke. But it was not smoke; it was demon ghosts. The ghosts clustered in the outer area seemingly unable to move away from it and ignored the battle going on around them. Gallois realized with frightening certainty that the ghosts were watching him. The ghosts seemed to know that his reason for being there was different from the soldiers'. He did not see Sean anywhere, and despite himself he was relieved.

He tore his eyes from the ghost, spotted Malcolm, and flew down to him.

Malcolm's eyes were wild, and he sounded frantic. "Gallois! How are they doing up top?"

"They're on the middle level!" Gallois shouted, trying to be heard above the gunfire and demonic screams.

Malcolm checked his weapon. There was only one ammo clip visible. "We're low on ammo. We didn't expect this many of them. There's no signal down here." He pointed up toward a skylight nearly hidden by earth. "Can you fly through that?"

Malcolm put a hand to a wound on his leg. "We're not going to last much longer. We're running out of ammo! We've dropped some charges inside the hole, but we don't have enough. I'm going blow it anyway. Listen. You've got to tell Hinshaw to send in the jets! Tell him level this whole building!" He pointed to the ceiling. "You think you can fly through that?"

Gallois studied the skylight. The dirt stained glass appeared to be thin. "Yes, bu—"

"Good! Fly through it, and tell Hinshaw that we've dropped the charges inside the pit. I don't think we have enough. I'm going to blow it anyway. Tell him to have the jets on standby. He should level this place to make sure."

Gallois noticed that Malcolm had not mentioned when they needed to leave.

"OK. I'll tell him," Gallois said "You should get out of here."

"We can't. The exit is blocked, and we're going to run out of ammo soon."

Gallois could not believe what he was hearing. Leaving them all to die was definitely not the plan. And where was Mermon? Gallois sensed the demon was near.

"No!" he said. "I'll tell him to send more soldiers. They'll be here; we just have to—".

Malcolm grabbed Gallois by his shirt. "We're too far down. We're not going to last long enough for them to get here. You have to do this! It's the only way."

Gallois looked at the break in the wall, pulled away from Malcolm, and took flight. He soared to the top of the concrete beam next to the break in the wall and wedged himself between them. He pushed with all the strength in his legs. After a few labored attempts, the beam cracked, and then it crumbled to the floor. The debris crushed most of the possessed and left a wave of dust that passed over the entire cavern. The soldiers were disoriented for a moment. Once they realized what had happened, they began firing on the remaining creatures.

After the last creature had fallen, the soldiers and Gallois gathered around Malcolm. Gallois looked around. The smoke demons had vanished, and there was still no sign of Mermon. He realized the soldiers were looking at him. They nodded in matter that seemed more like a salute which Gallois returned before looking at Malcolm.

Malcolm surveyed the room, hearing only the faint roars of the demons trapped underneath pieces of broken concrete. He pointed to a pair of steel doors on the other side of the room. "Check those," he ordered, and the soldiers sprinted toward the doors.

Danger!

Gallois' telepathy sent its chilling warning. He surveyed the room with dread, expecting to see Sean, not knowing how he was going to do what the angels had sent him to do.

"What's wrong?" Malcolm asked.

"You should hurry," Gallois answered despite not wanting to be left alone. Before Malcolm could reply, they heard a soldier announcing that two hostages had been found. They turned and saw soldiers emerging from the doors helping two men walk. Malcolm hurried over, and Gallois kept an eye on the cavern. He heard Malcolm say something, and then he heard a voice that he had thought he would never hear again. He swung around and felt his knees waken when he saw Ramiro limping from the steel doors. Their equally shocked eyes met, and Gallois wanted to run over and hug him as Malcolm was doing.

Gallois surveyed the room, paying particular attention to the entrance he'd closed with the fallen cylinder. "I don't know—we should hurry." That was putting it lightly after what they'd just been through the words would carry their own weight. They heard a soldier cry-out and both their heads spun around.

Before Gallois could move, the room began to shake and thousands of screams and bellows arouse from within the pit. He turned around just in time to see a cloud of demon ghosts erupting like lava from the pit. There were thousands of the ugly, nightmarish creatures. The hoard splashed onto the mounds of earth and the ceiling and then rained down on the cavern, scattering like angry bees. Their ghost bodies passed through every living body in the cavern. Gallois noticed trails of demons exiting the cavern through small cracks in the ceiling, while others vanished down the corridor.

Baffled and scared, Gallois and the soldiers watched in horror. The ghosts did not bother with them; their only concern seemed to be with escaping the cavern. A deafening roar sounded from the pit, and then a mammoth hand appeared at its edge. The hand was followed by bat like wings and a large arm and bald head with two black holes where eyes should have been. The soldiers were shooting before the creature could fully lift its nine-foot frame out of the pit. The soldiers were pulling Ramiro and the other rescued soldier out of the cavern; both of the men resisted and called out Gallois' name but were too injured to put up much of a fight as they were quickly dragged from the cavern.

As the remaining soldiers fired at the demon, golden specs of light that looked like tiny comets infiltrated the room from every possible direction and quickly gave chase to the ghost demons. Once one of the golden lights seized a ghost demon, it morphed into an angel ghost and delivered a killing blow with a sword. Then the angel returned to light and pursued another demon. But there wasn't time to stare at the ghostly battle; Mermon had cleared the pit. The demon roared, and it sounded like there was more than one of him. The creature stood with its arms spread wide, baring its jagged teeth. Bullets tore into the creature's flesh with wet sounds as they hit their mark and sent pieces of skin flying. The beast charged at him with heavy steps, moving much faster than something of its size should.

Gallois picked up an M16 from the ground and aimed it at the demon. He fired, but the gun was empty. He leaped and flew backwards just in time to avoid the beast's massive fist. He landed behind Malcolm and the soldiers who had already advanced. The soldiers' aim was precise. But even shots to the beast's head didn't kill it, and it was on top of them in seconds. Malcolm pulled Gallois away as the creature swung and sent the soldiers flying.

Before Malcolm could waste time using his handgun, Gallois grabbed the army knife from his west and flew toward

Mermon with his sights on the beast's throat. Before reaching his target, he felt the weight of something drop down onto him and tumbled to the ground. He landed a few feet in front of Mermon. He fought off fangs and soon realized that the fangs reaching for his neck belonged to Leba. After two failed attempts, it settled for his shoulder. Gallois felt the crushing pressure of the bite, but his shirt was not punctured.

He swung the knife and managed to drive the blade deep into Leba's thigh but the beast did not release its hold. Mermon reached them and slammed its fists down onto both of them and sent them to the ground hard. The force took the air out of Gallois. Leba was still on top of him. The demon's body had shielded him from the full force of the blow a seemingly killed it. Gallois could feel the creature's broken bones poking him in the back. Not able to breathe or move, Gallois could only watch as the beast raised its foot. Malcolm and two other soldiers fired rounds into the creature's back, but that did not stop Mermon. The creature kicked him in the face. White light flashed. The next thing he knew he was awakening in another spot on the cavern floor with his face in the dirt.

He heard Malcolm yelling. The side of his face was numb with pain; blood poured from his mouth; his neck felt broken. He felt Mermon's giant hand grab him, and then he saw the beast's leg as it lifted him. Something gold struck the creature in the back. Blood sprayed down onto his face. He turned away and was grateful for the pain because it meant his neck wasn't broken. Mermon dropped him but then fell on top of him, pinning his lower body.

Gallois tried to free himself, but the creature was too heavy. At the sound of Malcolm's voice, he looked at the soldiers moving in his direction. Golden light flashed in front of them. When the light vanished, Khama was standing there. Malcolm and the soldiers were visibly awestruck. The angel said something to them and then morphed back into light. With slight hesitation, Malcolm pointed toward the exit, and one of the soldiers handed him what appeared to be a detonator before following the other to the corridor.

Mermon slowly began to move again. Gallois saw Malcolm looking at him with his hand on the detonator. Gallois knew what needed to happen. He knew Malcolm wanted his permission. He stopped moving and gave into the fate the detonator held for him. He nodded. He could see the soldier fighting with himself before turning and looking at him one last time before exiting the cavern.

Gallois did not have long to wait for the horrible end. Within seconds, there was a huge explosion from within the pit. The shockwave shook the ground so hard that it freed him from the demon. The ground quaked, but he somehow managed to get to his feet. Cracks trailed from the pit to the walls and concrete, and then the cavern began to collapse. The edge of the pit began to fall away, and the rest of ground followed as slabs of concrete and dirt rained down, crushing the ground and corpses. Gallois looked at the passage that led to the corridor and saw that it had already collapsed. He heard Khama's voice call to him, "Fly Gallois!"

He looked up at the skylight through the falling debris and thrust himself into the air. Once aloft, he heard Mermon following him. He did not look down' doing so meant that he would certainly be crushed by falling concrete. He flew as fast as he dared, hoping not to be grabbed. Finally, with dirt stinging at his eyes, the skylight came into view. He covered his face and broke through the glass.

Then he looked down, expecting to see Mermon. But all he saw was a cloud of dirt. The demon had not been as lucky. He let out a sigh of relief, but he could not take his eyes off of the skylight. He mouthed the words, "it's over," though he did not accept the idea until he thought of Ramiro. He spoke into the communicator, "General, can you hear me?"

Henshaw did not respond. He felt his ear The earpiece was gone. He looked around, trying to determine how far away he was from the group. All he saw was a swamp below him, the city in the distance.

Danger!

He heard the sound of breaking glass. When he looked down, he saw Mermon flying up after him.

He flew toward the city. The creature gained on him despite appearing more injured than he was. He led the demon into a forest of palm trees. He hoped the leaves would help him lose the beast in the darkness. But there was no such luck. The trees did not even slow the creature down; it broke what it could not avoid and stayed close enough that Gallois could hear its horse-like breathing. He looked to his right and saw a highway. The choice was clear. He could not worry about being seen if he wanted to survive. He banked a hard left and followed the highway. They flew above traffic and caused as many car cashes as they did screams.

They entered the city. Gallois' lungs and back were on fire. He could not maintain the speed that had gotten him there. Flying erratically was all he could do to avoid capture. He rounded buildings, often barely missing head-on collisions with billboards. The near misses gave him an idea. He swerved and then flew up alongside two adjoining buildings with an overpass. There was only enough space for him to get through. He angled through the gap, and Mermon crashed.

Masonry and glass were still falling as Gallois hovered up alongside the wreckage, hoping Mermon was dead. He moved closer, trying to see through the wreckage. Wires popped and sparked. Mermon suddenly emerged from the wreckage and tackled him. They fought as their bodies fell from the sky until they landed on a news van.

The van was crushed on the impact that rendered both of them still. Wrapped in paralyzing pain, Gallois opened his eyes and saw the sky and the place from which they had fallen. The beast was not moving either. It had landed beside him, its hand still around his neck. He pulled Mermon's long fingers away and made the painful effort of moving. He crawled from the wreckage on his hands and knees. He heard whispers and looked up at the dozens of eyes staring back at him from behind parked cars. He kept his eyes on the people as he struggled to his feet

He watched the people, expecting them to attack at any moment. He flexed the muscles in his back. He could still fly if he needed to. He slowly looked over his shoulder at Mermon. What he saw relieved him and made him want to vomit at the same time. The creature's neck had been broke by a folded piece of metal.

"You getting this?" a man dressed in a suit and tie said to another man holding a strange object on his shoulder. Gallois looked at the object and realized that the circular thing he was staring into was a camera. He arched his wings and prepared to take fight.

Danger!

Gallois heard a noise coming from the van and turned around to see Mermon's broken body twitching. The creature's mouth fell open, and black smoke arose from it. The smoke smelled like something dead. It coalesced into a demonic ghost that was even scarier than Mermon; it looked like a cross between an angel and goat. The people gasped and ducked further into their hiding spots.

The smoke swelled before him like a cobra raising its hood. It fell over him like steam. He swung at the ghost, and his fist went through the ghost's body. Smoke trailed into his nostrils and burned as it took away oxygen. He flapped his wings and pushed himself away from the figure, but it stayed on him. He gasped for air and found none.

In desperation, he picked up a newspaper box and threw it. The box sailed through the ghost. Thinking there was no other choice, he fled into the air. The ghostly figure followed. It moved so fast, skipping though the air as if it were teleporting. Gallois flew as fast as his injures would allow. He searched the ground for any place to escape. But there was nothing below except a grassy field, and it was already too late. The ghost had engulfed his body.

Smoke trailed back into his nose and mouth. He coughed out the last bit of air in his lungs. Pressure gradually intensified in his chest. He pulled his wings close to his body, hoping the dive would cause the demon to lose its hold on him. He descended fast, but not fast enough to shake the demon. He reached the ground and landed on his hands and knees. There was pressure in his head now too, and the veins behind his eyes already felt like they would explode. He swiped at his mouth and nose, but his hand still went through the trail of smoke. He fell over in the grass, surrounded by the demon's heat and paralyzed by pain. He wanted to scream for help. He would scream for Khama. His thought rushed despite the consuming pain as if his brain were trying to make sense of what was about to happen. Was this the angel's plan all along? Do I need to die to kill Mermon? Helpless and alone, he stared through blades of grass, drowning in his final thoughts.

He heard a swooshing sound like wind blowing through trees, and suddenly the heat lifted and he could breathe again. His body greedily drew in air as he searched for the demon, fearing that it had stopped in favor of killing him another way. He saw the ghost standing several feet away, enclosed in a circle by Khama and six other angels. The angels' eyes shone against the night as they stared at the demon in angry triumph. The demon cowered before them. The sight of the bigger, scarier being afraid of the smaller, prettier ones was like seeing a serpent afraid of an eagle. Khama said something to the demon that

Gallois missed over the sound of his own breathing. However, it enraged the demon. Anger shifted on the creature's face as it yelled at the angels in a voice that sounded like howling wind.

The angels were indifferent to the demon's yelling. They raised their arms, and the ghost grew even more frantic. It bared its ghostly fangs and stomped the ground, disturbing it even though the demon did not have a physical body. The demon began to sink into the ground like quicksand. The creature thrashed about desperately trying to stop its decent. When its chest reached the ground, it seemed to finally accept its fate and stopped resisting. It stared at the angels in a hateful way that would surely haunt Gallois' dreams before it vanished beneath the dirt.

When the demon was gone, the angels gathered behind Khama and walked over to Gallois. He wanted to get to his feet, but his was dizzy and his legs would not move. He felt as if he had been beaten with a branding rod and left beneath something heavy. With the assistance of Khama, he clumsily got to his feet.

"Is it over?" he asked wearily as he stared at the disturbed grass behind the angels.

Khama's gaze was full of empathy, "Yes."

Gallois sighed and collapsed into the angel's arms, briefly losing consciousness before awakening on the ground with the angel's arms still around him. He opened his eyes and saw the angels looking down at him. In the haze of exhaustion, he feared that he had dreamed everything and would soon awaken surrounded by glass walls.

He grabbed Khama's arm. "You're real," he said.

The angel nodded. "You did well. The Nesphar will never again trouble your family. You have the peace you wanted."

As Gallois struggled to imagine his life without worrying about the Nesphar, Khama looked up. Gallois followed his gaze and saw the headlights of fast-approaching vehicles in the distance. Gallois heard Khama tell him that his friends were coming. When he turned his head, the angels had vanished, leaving him to wonder if he would ever see them again.

Chapter 24

Three days later.

THE LAST RAYS of sunlight shone on the desert as Ramiro stood with his right arm around Lisa's shoulder. His other arm was in a sling. The watched Hinshaw's soldiers as they loaded the last boxes of cargo onto the jumbo plane, while Malcolm and Dr. Klein stood nearby saying their final goodbyes to Hinshaw. A shadow passed over him and his daughter. They turned their heads upward and saw Gallois gliding out into the desert. Ramiro smiled and pulled his daughter closer. "I've never seen him so happy," Ramiro said.

"He deserves it," Lisa said, "He and his mother. Where is she, anyway? I've hardly seen her since we got back."

"She's been looking after the soldier we brought back. He's eager to get back on his feet. She's been helping him along."

"After all you two have been through, he should be taking his time," Lisa said.

Ramiro grinned. "I think he'll rest after today."

Lisa's expression was puzzled. "What's happening today?"

"I'll tell you later," Ramiro said. He smiled and kissed her now wrinkled forehead. They turned and saw Klein approaching with an aggravated expression.

"Are you okay, Doctor?" Lisa asked. Klein's face hardened as she stood with them, folded her arms, and scowled in the direction of the plane.

"He couldn't just leave without one last jab at me," Klein hissed.

"What do you mean?" Ramiro asked.

"He's taking the bodies."

"You mean the bodies of the possessed?" Lisa asked.

Klein looked at her as if she had said something in a foreign language. "Um, yes. He said the Vatican wanted them." She exhaled, and it sounded like the beginnings of a curse word. "We all know that it's really the military that wants them. They're always looking for that next weapon."

Ramiro looked at the loaded cargo. He did not want to believe that Hinshaw would allow anyone to weaponized the evil they had witnessed. He would not take the chance of being wrong. At that moment he decided he was going to have the bodies followed, and if Henshaw had lied to him, he was going to send soldiers in to destroy the bodies.

He told Klein only, "I assure you, Doctor, those corpses are going to be incinerated."

There was a spark of hope in her eyes. He could see her forming the words for asking him to keep one of the corpses for research. He turned away before she could. He would not be able to sleep knowing one of those things was around. He felt the doctor watching him, but she did not ask. Instead, she checked the stitches above his left eye, and it hurt.

"It's healing well," she said. "I thought there was going to be some nerve damage."

"He's a tough old man," Lisa said with a grin.

"Apparently. He's healing almost as fast as Gallois, whom I haven't seen in two days."

"We saw him fly by a few minutes ago," Lisa said.

Klein removed her hand from Ramiro's bandage. "What did the Vatican say we should do about him? The cameraman that saw him that night is all over the TV trying to convince people that his footage of Gallois is real."

Ramiro gave her a long look. "I won't have him locked away again. I've ordered a restricted area radius of ten miles around this place. He'll be safe out there." He wanted to believe that was the truth. He needed it to be.

Gallois arched his wings and landed on a boulder at the edge of a valley in the desert. He took a moment and surveyed his surroundings. When he was sure no one was watching, he turned his gaze to the horizon and marveled at the beauty before him. The sun was setting, causing the sky to fade to soothing shades of gold and burgundy that made the sand appear red as darkness leaned on the shadows of the bushes and Joshua trees.

Minutes passed. When the sun began to descend below the horizon, angels appeared on the surrounding boulders and gazed at the sun with him. Gallois watched them and felt a surreal feeling of gratitude and inferiority in the presence of the righteous beings. He wanted to be worthy of their attention, to achieve the smallest measure of devotion to the goodness they represented.

When the sun set, the angels vanished. He flew back to the Oasis thinking about them. By the time he neared the Facility, the idea of fight alongside the angels had fully formed in his mind. He was pondering how he would ask Khama when he neared the roof and saw two people sitting in lawn chairs near the access door. He flew closer and saw one was his mother. The other he vaguely recognized as the soldier they had rescued with Ramiro two days ago. His mother roused from the chair as he landed on the railing and stepped down onto the roof. His mother's arm was round the soldier's shoulder. The man was so thin that the bones in his face showed, and the army t-shirt and fatigues he wore hung loosely on him. Both the man and his mother were smiling, but there were tears in their eyes.

"Hi, baby," his mother said in a shaky voice.

Confused, and thinking the worst, Gallois watched and waited to hear the awful news. His mouth had gone dry when he spoke, "What's wrong?" he asked.

His mother started crying, as did the soldier as he wrapped his arm around her waist. His mother leaned over onto the man as if she were the one inured. "Nothing," she finally said. "Nothing at all. Everything is going to be fie from now on."

She wept more and looked down at the soldier. The man wiped the tears from her cheek, and their foreheads touched as they hugged. Gallois studied the man's face and wondered if he were a distant friend that his mother had never mentioned. She reached for him and told him to come to her. He walked over as she smiled again. He saw the joy in her eyes that he had always wanted to see, and it made his eyes well-up too. He thought of something to say to avoid crying.

"He's getting better," Gallois managed.

His mother sniffled. "Yes he is. We'll have him walking soon." She looked at the man and then at him. "I was just telling him about you and how you volunteered to help the Knights fight the demons. He was very impressed."

"He fought them too." Gallois replied.

"Yes, he did." She looked down at the soldier. "You both are brave." She turned back to him. "I'm going down stairs and prepare dinner." She walked over to the access door and looked back at him. "Can you help him down when you come?" Gallois nodded with raised eyebrows. He could feel the soldier looking at him but didn't know what to say.

His mother pulled open the access door and held it open as she looked back at them. "Oh. I almost forgot to introduce you two. Fabian, this is Gallois. Gallois, say hello to your father."